Bu

Book One

Love That House

Building of the Kingdom

Book One

Love That House

By

R.M. Rogers

Building of the Kingdom

Book One: Love That House
Book Two: Singing Windows
Book Three: Home of the Bears

Desert Breeze Publishing, Inc.
27305 W. Live Oak Rd #424
Castaic, CA 91384

http://www.DesertBreezePublishing.com

Copyright © 2016 by R.M. Rogers
ISBN 13: 978-1-68294-924-5

Published in the United States of America
Publication Date: November 2016

Editor-In-Chief: Gail R. Delaney
Editor: Shawna Williams
Marketing Director: Jenifer Ranieri
Cover Artist: Carol Fiorillo

Cover Art Copyright by Desert Breeze Publishing, Inc © 2016

All rights reserved. No portion of this book may be reproduced or transmitted in any form or by any electronic or mechanical means, including photocopying, recording or by any information retrieval and storage system without permission of the publisher.

Names, characters and incidents depicted in this book are products of the author's imagination, or are used in a fictitious situation. Any resemblances to actual events, locations, organizations, incidents or persons – living or dead – are coincidental and beyond the intent of the author.

Dedication and Acknowledgment

For Vic, who steps up to the hard jobs.

Thanks to Pat, Joe, and editor Shawna Williams.

Chapter One

Port Tiffany, Washington State

Collin sat quietly in front of the computer. This was what Jan had wanted for him. This was what they had planned for and worked for -- early retirement, their beautiful daughter in college, a cottage in the Pacific Northwest, and time for Collin to sail and write his book. Jan, from her heavenly place, was surely smiling at him now. So, why couldn't he write? Where were the words? Maybe if he ate something it would help. He went to the kitchen where he made a sandwich with leftover meatloaf and slices of tomato, and then sat down at the table and read the newspaper as he ate.

He brought his plate to the sink when he finished, and as he washed it, glanced frequently through the kitchen window at the house next door. She usually appeared on her back porch every evening, her frail 92-year-old-body moving slowly and carefully. Collin poured a cup of coffee into his mug, and by the time he turned back around she was seating herself in front of the climbing yellow rose bush.

He needed to get back to his book, to actually start the book, rather than peering out the window at and keeping track of an elderly woman. But he liked his new neighbor and found her to be pleasant company. Deep within his soul, he suspected that somehow, in this phase of their lives, they needed each other.

So, here he was, in a new-to-him cottage, with his boat visible, moored in the harbor, and beyond that the blue gray waters of the Strait of Juan de Fuca and the Townsend Islands beyond. A good setup for the next part of his life, a life concentrating on writing a book, but he would put off starting that book one more time. What he saw in front of him was an old lady who needed some company.

He crossed the grass between the two houses, and stood at the bottom of her steps.

"Permission to come aboard?" he asked.

"For you? Always!"

He settled into the chair beside her and placed his mug on the wrought iron table between them.

As she looked toward the water, he gazed at her profile, her chiseled straight nose and her high forehead with her gray hair pulled back in a bun. She looked like a picture from the 1900s, sitting among the pots of blooming plants and the climbing yellow rose. He didn't know her well but he liked listening to her talk about the history of the area. Most of her friends were gone, but she didn't complain. There was an elegance about her that he liked.

She smiled. "With all that you do for people and the things you take care of -- your sailboat and sailing are never far from your thoughts, are they, Collin?"

"It's true. The water and the boats, my boat in particular, give me great joy."

He watched May lift her cup of tea with both hands to control the tremors. She held it close to her nose, her eyes closed, as she enjoyed the fragrance of the tea. After sipping it, she then looked at him. "I do have a problem I hope you can help me with."

Before he could answer, a figure emerged from behind the climbing rose bush, startling both of them.

"Hello! I tried the front door bell, but no one answered," said the man with a friendly smile.

"Pastor Andy! Come sit down and meet my new neighbor," said May.

Andy, tall and thin, quickly folded his lanky body into a chair, and got to the point. "May, I know you're a long-time church member of another church, and I recall your saying you preferred not to be active in a church, but I just wanted you to know you would be welcome at my church anytime."

She nodded and then said, "Thank you. I'll think about it. I'm sure the music and the worship services have changed a lot from what I'm used to."

He continued on. "I'm not pushy, but please remember that I, the church, cares about you and if there is anything we can do for you, please please let us know."

"I certainly will. I'm steady-state right now." After the three of them exchanged pleasantries, Andy pointed to the harbor.

"If my small-town information track is right, you have a sailboat tied up down there," he said.

"Your sources are correct, and if you're interested, maybe when she's seaworthy you'd like to go sailing." It was odd for Collin to say this, because he didn't want to set himself up to be proselytized, but he liked this young man, and it blurted out in a spontaneous, unusual way.

Andy left as quickly as he came. Collin thought about how May had treated the pastor cordially but coolly. He wondered about that, and kept quiet, to see if she wanted to talk about the pastor, the church, or religion, but she said nothing.

"May, you wanted to talk about something before Andy showed up. I hope I can help. What's on your mind?"

She looked out at the horizon before she answered.

"I'm an old lady now, and most of my friends are gone and I didn't have any children. I don't know who to leave my property to."

Collin squirmed as much as his 220 pounds could squirm in the chair.

"May, it seems to me that you likely have a cause you would want to leave your property to. Possibly some organization here in town. Maybe the church?"

She waved her hand dismissively. "Yes, there's the church, but I haven't been active recently. My friends have died off. I suppose my friend Jared James, one of the few remaining oldsters still around, the director down at the museum -- he would love to have my property."

And it must be worth a pretty penny, thought Collin. This cottage overlooking the harbor and within walking distance into town should be quite valuable.

"That sounds like it has possibilities," he said amiably.

"No, it doesn't. Sounds awful to me. But I know he wants it. He's been friendly recently, claiming a long-time friendship between us, but deep in my heart I'm pretty sure he just wants the property to help fund his beloved museum."

Collin shrugged. "Okay. Maybe you have a distant relative."

"I have a great-niece I've never met. She's an artist in Santa Fe."

"That sounds promising," said Collin.

"I don't think so. She doesn't sound like much to me. I also have a great-nephew, on my brother's side of the family. He's made it big in New York -- as a stockbroker. And as for friends in this town, I hope you never have to face the betrayal that I have had to face in our quiet little town. I wish for you lots of dependable friends here in Port Tiffany. My problems here will die with me."

She put down her cup and took hold of his hand. Collin held it gently, afraid of hurting the fragile bones and the transparent skin.

"I would like to invite my great-nephew, HH, short for Herbert Humphrey, and my great-niece, Julie, to come visit this summer. I don't know them and I'd like to, with decisions to make and all."

"That's sounds like a good plan." What else could he say?

"She could stay here with me, and we could get to know each other. HH actually has a house up on the bluff, the house he grew up in. They visit once in a while. If they come this summer, maybe I could have a chance to get a better opinion of him and of her."

"Well--"

"Collin, how long do you think I'll live?"

"At ninety-two, you are definitely on the short side of life, but you look good to go to me." That was a lie. She looked especially pale in the evening light, but she smiled at the compliment.

"I hope so," she said. "I don't know what I'm supposed to do with the rest of my life. I feel there is some purpose, something God wants me to do. Do you believe in God, Collin?"

"I do. I will admit, besides writing a book, I don't know what I'm supposed to be doing either. Retired early and life looks like a blank canvas. I haven't gone to church in a long time."

Like since Jan's funeral, he thought, but May's voice brought him back to the present.

"My birthday is the last day of June I'd like to have a party, and invite Jared, and HH, and Julie, and some other local people. The pastor perhaps. He's sort of growing on me, even though I don't want to go to his church, or any church for that matter. Would you help me with that?"

This is exactly the kind of involvement he didn't want. He would rather shoot himself in the foot than be involved in this party or those people. "Sounds interesting, May. Let me think about it. I might be out sailing."

She smiled brightly. "Would you like to play some cards with me? That will keep your brain working while God comes up with the bigger plans."

"Sure. You want to go inside where it's warmer?"

"No. If you will go into the middle bedroom, my sewing room, you will see my shawl on the bed. That will do, and bring the deck of cards on the kitchen table. Thank you."

The middle bedroom jarred his mind. She used it as a sewing room, but still, for anyone to be so organized about her own appearance and her home, and then have such a room in her house was beyond understanding. Collin couldn't even see what it all was, but stuff, maybe old greeting cards, clippings from newspapers and magazines, and who knew what else, pinned all over the walls. Everywhere. He found the shawl on the single bed and backed out of the room.

He couldn't find the deck of cards on the kitchen table. "May, I'm not finding the cards," he said loudly.

No answer. He looked all over the kitchen counter and still couldn't find them. Giving up, he walked to the back door to get more directions. "May?" he asked as he opened the door.

May lay sprawled on the porch, her tea cup broken beside her.

Chapter Two

Everything hooked up to May either beeped, blinked, or burbled. He had survived his wife's death and thought he would never have to experience this again, but here he was. It wasn't as if he had known May a long time, or that they were close, but still, here he was, in the most intimate of experiences, and all he could do was stare down at May and wonder about it all. What was he supposed to do?

A small blond nurse appeared next to him. When Collin bent down to look at her name tag, he saw she was pregnant. "Ms. Moore, what happens next?"

"You can call me Angie. She's stable now. You can go home and get some rest. Our specialist will want to see you in the morning. Early."

"I'm just a neighbor--."

"You'll do for now. Get some sleep."

The long evening was not over yet. Collin returned to May's house and found May's purse on her desk. He opened it and retrieved her house keys, checked the back door and the windows, and then left by the front door, locking it. Before he had gone down the steps, he turned, reopened the door, picked up May's purse, and then locked up and went to his own home to get some sleep. If God really did exist, why the hell was he in this situation again? It wasn't fair. He'd done his time.

*****

The spring night in Seattle, although dark, noisy with traffic, and misty damp, still held the fresh vague scent of trees blooming. Sandy Matthews parked her car, retrieved the painting from the trunk, dodged past couples standing in line to get into the University Bistro and then entered into the serene St. Francis University campus, where lights gently lit the pathways and gardens; the mixture of old brick buildings and new sculpted buildings created ethereal canyons. Compared to the busy city sidewalks, the university paths were quiet, but Sandy knew when she got to the art gallery, she would find people working to get ready for the art show opening. She hurriedly moved along, carrying the painting in front of her.

When she first noticed the footsteps behind her, she was not concerned, but she became nervous listening to the steps, and when she stopped, the steps behind her stopped. Sandy peered into the darkness, but couldn't see anyone. She started walking again and when she sped up, the steps came faster.

Sandy didn't run, but walked faster and faster, and she heard the steps coming closer and closer. Her heart pounded in her chest. If she could just get around the corner, she could see the gallery and there would be people on the promenade. She started to run as fast as she could, holding the painting and being careful where she stepped. When she reached the corner, she turned, slipped, and fell, hitting her head. She saw the painting still in her hands and breathed her relief before blackness consumed her.

*****

"Sandy? Sandy? Are you okay?"
Sandy looked up into the familiar eyes of Dean Hopkins as he leaned over her. She didn't remember who he was at first, or where she was and what she was doing. "What are you doing here?" she asked. "Where am I?"
"Just stay quiet," he said. "We'll talk later. The main thing is I'm here. Everything's going to be okay." He sat down beside her.
She swallowed hard, and thought she tasted blood. She fought the urge to get up and get moving. Lying on the sidewalk with the dean sitting beside her didn't seem right, but the thought of moving made her nauseous. The more she became conscious, the more she was aware of Dean Hopkins' calm presence, and she became less interested in moving. She didn't have to move. He just continued sitting there, not talking. The in and out of her own breath, the stars, the light from the street lamp over the dean's shoulder -- all slowly came into focus.
"Is the painting okay?" she asked.
"I don't know, Sandy. Who cares? Lie still and don't move. I'll get you to the infirmary."
"No. No. Just help me sit up."
He helped her sit up and moved behind her to support her back. "What happened? I saw you running. Was somebody chasing you?"
"I think so. I'm not sure. I was scared. I can't remember. All I know is my head hurts."
"Do you think you can walk? Test everything before you get up."
She stretched her legs and wiggled her toes, then moved her arms, her neck, and leaned to the right and the left. "I'm okay. Really. I want to stand up. Even my head hurts less. She reached up to touch the area. It stung and felt wet. Sandy quickly withdrew her hand, shocked by the sight of her bloody finger tips.
He helped Sandy up, steadying her as she stood and looked around. "On this campus, of all places, everyone should feel safe. I'm so sorry I asked you to go get the painting," he said.
She took one step and then another.
"Let's get over to the gallery if you can walk, and see if you need to go to the infirmary."

Love that House

The work of setting up the first faculty art show in the history of the university stopped as Dean Hopkins walked in with a battered Sandy Matthews. Eased into a chair, Sandy struggled to stay conscious while students and faculty surrounded her.

"She needs to go to the infirmary," said Dean Hopkins as he peered at the bloody wound on her head.

"No, really," protested Sandy.

"Yes, really," said several in the group.

"Should we call your parents?" asked the dean.

"No, no, no," said Sandy. "I'll go to the infirmary, but I think they'll say I'm fine and no need to call my dad. He's just started his retirement and I don't want to bother him."

*****

The next morning Collin told his story to a doctor young enough to be his son. "I'm her neighbor -- she didn't have any children. Last night, right before this happened, she told me she didn't have anybody close to her, just a great niece in Santa Fe and a great nephew in New York, and she didn't think much of either of them," said Collin. The doctor frowned at him. No doubt the doctor would like this situation to be tidier. So would Collin, and as soon as he could get himself out of it, he would not look back.

"Look," said the doctor, "She's lived in this town a long time and I know she's old, but there needs to be some decisions made here. She's got to have someone around who can make decisions."

Collin remembered May saying something about an old friend. Who was it? Something to do with the manager of the museum.

"I'm new to the area, but she had just confided in me yesterday that the director of the museum is an old friend."

The doctor looked at him quizzically. "Jared James?"

"That's it!" said Collin.

"Okay then," said the doctor. "Get him in here. We need to make some decisions. Get in touch with that niece and nephew. While you're at it, look for any papers in her desk, or safe or wherever that designates a person to make health care decisions."

*****

Collin started up the steps to the museum briskly and with enthusiasm, but when he reached the top, he stopped, breathing heavily to catch his breath, and then after a few moments, he opened the heavy double doors and entered the cool, dark, sedate museum, a place with dignity most small town Carnegie museums had and he never tired of.

At the end of the hall sat a woman with frizzy hair and too much makeup. As he approached she pointed at the admission fee sign and then at the box on her desk.

"I need to see Jared James," he said.

She pointed behind herself at an open office door.

Collin knocked and peered in. A wiry older man stood by the window, looking at a rock in one hand and holding his glasses in the other hand. "Jared James?"

Jared James put his glasses on and asked, "And who are you?"

"I'm May Riley's next door neighbor. I believe you're an old friend of hers?"

Jared's face came alive. "What's happened to her?"

"I'm not sure, but she's in the hospital and the doctor would like you to come. She may have had a stroke."

Jared James moved past Collin before Collin finished his sentence.

*****

The doctor completed his exam of May and then stepped back to talk with Jared and Collin.

"Jared," said the doctor. "She did have a stroke, and now we have some decisions to make. Are you authorized to make any decisions about her health care?"

"No. She never mentioned anything about that to me. But can I talk to her?"

"I suppose," said the doctor. "She is in a coma. Be brief and positive. We really do have some decisions to make." He turned to Collin. "Did you have a chance to contact those relatives or check her papers for any authorizations about her health care?"

"No. I'm going to her house now. I'll find the information about the niece and nephew I mentioned earlier," said Collin.

Jared snorted. "That niece is a worthless woman who never showed any interest in May."

"Mr. James, she can hear you. Knock it off," said the doctor.

Collin glared at him, knowing that May didn't trust Jared and his interest in her.

Collin and the doctor stood by while Jared sat down and took May's hand in his.

"May? May?"

She moved her head slightly and Jared looked at the doctor questioningly. The doctor said nothing but watched her intently.

"May. It's Jared. For Pete's sake don't leave now, May. I'm not ready. You're not ready. You know what I'm talking about. May, I am willing you to live. With all my heart and soul, May, with every ounce of energy in my body, I am willing you to live."

She moved her head again.

8

Jared bowed his head, and Collin wondered if he was praying. The doctor left, but Collin waited. He would wait and leave after Jared did. The undercurrent of drama Jared James carried with him puzzled Collin, and he wanted to make sure none of it settled on to May behind his back. He may be the newcomer in town, but May trusted him and he would not let her down. There would be plenty of time to track down the niece and nephew. If anybody could go through someone else's desk fast and get the business at hand organized, it was him, Collin Matthews, businessman extraordinaire.

Chapter Three

Santa Fe, New Mexico

Julie stormed along, her sandals missing all the cracks and uneven sidewalk edges. She did not stop at the corner, but glanced around for traffic and marched by the plaza in the center of Santa Fe and then down the side street, full of tourists and the shops geared to appeal to them and lighten their wallets. On this day, Julie was not envious, not envious of their clean new cars and she was certainly not envious of the ability they had to seriously look at the jewelry and the tooled leather goods that sparkled in the shop windows. She was focused and did not envy.

At the church, instead of going in the main door, she grabbed the basement door and floated down the steps, the door banging behind her. The stairs descended to a room with cinderblock walls and gray indoor/outdoor carpeting. Julie skipped exchanging pleasantries with the other people gathered there and headed straight for the coffee.

For most of the hour she sat, with a cup of coffee in hand, and struggled to listen to the others. She couldn't hold back her own intruding thoughts and it added to her frustration. She reminded herself why she was there -- they all were there.

Now, Julie couldn't hear anything anyone else said because of the anger buzzing in her head, but she heard the lull, the quiet, that meant she could speak, and then she said, "I'm Julie, I come to these meetings because you're the only people I can be honest with, and I want you to know I hate tomatoes and peppers." She took a deep breath. "I'm an artist. I make a living by painting insipid cute pictures of food for restaurants -- their advertising and their menus."

Julie looked around the room. They all sat quietly and listened, which was what she wanted and needed. She needed to say it out loud, the frustration she felt with her life, and not have anyone tell her she shouldn't feel that way. She did feel that way. Faye, her best friend, knew the protocol, and let Julie vent without comment. "But," she continued, "I'm sick of it, so totally sick of it I wish I could go to a bar and have a Margarita -- or go shopping. I'd love to have a leather jacket. There are days when I think the quality of my life would improve enormously if I owned a leather jacket. I know that isn't the answer. I won't do that. I'm not going to get mind altered with anything, including a leather jacket."

She looked around the room. She didn't say anything else. A handful of people said, "Thanks, Julie." And the silence began again, as they waited for the next person to speak.

Julie's phone vibrated as she sat there listening to the last speaker. She didn't recognize the ID, Collin Matthews. Who was that and who cared?

After the meeting, she picked up her purse and turned to leave. Faye, busy talking with two newcomers, waved at her -- they would talk later, but Ricardo stepped in front of her.

The red bandana tied low on his forehead accentuated his dark and foreboding eyes.

"You shouldn't tell so much about the personal details of your life," he said. "Nobody cares, and you're still better off than most of the people in here."

Julie's adrenalin rose to the occasion. "I don't care what you think," she said. "This is a place where I'm supposed to be free to say what I want." She almost jabbed him with her finger but didn't.

She saw through his tough exterior and into his confusion. He didn't think she would stand up to him. They stared at each other until he gave in. He moved to let her get by.

"Asshole," she said under her breath.

"What?" he asked.

"I said nobody asked you to be the thought police in here," She looked around defiantly and then left the basement, flounced up the stairs and headed home.

Inside her tiny apartment, Julie lit the kiva fireplace, poured herself the fifth cup of coffee of the day and sat down to look at her portfolio. Tomorrow was the day. The day she would hear from Atir Cards and her future depended on them saying they liked her work. A contract with Atir would mean painting more than fruits and vegetables. It would mean painting scenery and people -- a broader scope of images that would mean something to her, and the money would be much better than what she made now. She needed new challenges and money wouldn't hurt.

Her phone vibrated again and she saw the same name, Collin Matthews. With an exasperated sigh Julie answered, with as terse a hello as she could manage.

"Julie, you don't know me, but I'm your Great Aunt May's next door neighbor here in Washington State."

Silence. "Julie?"

"Yes, well, you caught me off guard. I've never met her. She and my mother weren't close. And why are you calling me?"

"Well, we both live here in Port Tiffany, that's on the Olympic Peninsula—"

"I know where it is."

"--and I haven't known her long, but she is in a bad way, and the doctor asked me to give you a call and ask you to come to Port Tiffany for a visit."

"Are you kidding me? I don't know her, I have a life, and I am actually expecting another very important call tomorrow. I can't imagine being necessary in her life."

"She's had a stroke, and it looks pretty serious. The doctors wanted to know if you could come for a visit."

"To do what?" Julie could not control her frustration.

"Possibly help make some decisions."

Silence. Then Julie said, "I don't know her well enough to make any decisions for her or with her. Call somebody else." She hung up the phone.

The next morning Julie awakened to robins singing, and for a brief moment she was still and peaceful, but then she remembered the expected phone call from New York. She needed to remember and apply everything she had ever learned about positive thinking. She lay there, using her breathing techniques and visualizing the contract, the new contract with Atir Cards. She could see herself receiving the contract in the mail, opening it, the joy that she would feel when she signed it. This was fun. Her life would change, she could see herself living not just in a small apartment, but in a house, with a garden, a new car. She could see her bank account ballooning so much that the banker would treat her with much more respect.

The images kept coming as Julie fixed her coffee and sat down at her drawing board. She could see the work she would do, the breadth of it, and her fame as an artist growing. She could see and enjoyed seeing all these things so much that she forgot the importance of the day. But the phone rang and she remembered instantly that no contract has been signed yet. She cleared her throat and picked up the phone. "Hello, Julie here."

"Julie Ashton?"

"Yes?" Was this the phone call she had been waiting for?"

"Julie, this is Greg Learner from Atir Cards. How are you today?"

And so it started, the phone call she had been waiting for, but it was different from what she expected. He didn't get right to the point of whether they liked her work or didn't. He wanted to chat, about art, and cards, and Julie participated as best she could, when she realized she was being interviewed, and she must participate and sound gracious and knowledgeable about beauty and the importance of cards in day-to-day life. And so they verbally danced for a few minutes and then he brought up her portfolio.

"Julie, we like your work, but we need to see more of it."

"I'd be happy to send you copies or originals of more of my work."

"That's not exactly what I had in mind," he said. "We would like to see you push yourself a little more."

"What does that mean?" she asked apprehensively.

"It means we would like for you to push yourself when it comes to landscapes. We'd like to see more understanding of color and depths when it comes to mountains, and trees, and water."

"Of course."

"In about a month, we would like to see 10 new paintings."

"I'd love to do that for you…"

"I'll talk to you again in about a month and see how that's coming. We like your work, but we really need to love it."

Graciously they both ended the phone call. Julie contemplated how the pleasant visualizations didn't work. She contemplated throwing something, like paint. They do that in the movies, cathartic moves, that release tension, but Julie could only think that if she threw paint at the walls it would be an expensive and time-consuming thing for her to fix.

Shit. Could nothing ever be simple and clear? Could nothing ever just come her way and be simple and charming, like other peoples' lives? Evidently not.

But, she could and would do what he asked. First thing would be to get in the shower and then put together her best watercolor supplies and drive to Taos. He wants mountains and water, she would give it to him and give it to him in glorious New Mexico colors. Rich tapestry-like greens, vibrant earth tones, and glorious sun-filled blues -- yes, she knew what to do.

Packed with art supplies, her tawny hair in a ponytail, and a ball cap to shield her eyes from the high altitude sun, Julie had just opened the door when the phone rang. What if it was Greg from Atir again? She let all of her supplies slide onto the floor and pulled her cell phone out of her pocket. It was that Collin guy from Washington State. She decided to not answer. She had nothing in common with this great aunt, and would not let anyone interfere with her life. She reached to place the phone in her jacket pocket as she knelt down to pick up her backpack and portable easel. Overly anxious to get started, Julie ignored the light clatter of something hitting the floor.

Julie hardly noticed the drive through Santa Fe, as she left town and headed north, but she knew what she was feeling, and it was a mixture of grief and fear, all rolled into one. Fear that life would overtake her and there was nothing she could do about it, there would never be enough positive thinking. Life would continue to be full of waves, some larger than others, and they would continue, beating her down, beating down her hope and spirit until there was nothing left.

By the time she had turned east to go up into the mountains, Julie found a small shred of positive thinking. It wasn't thoughts really, but determination, and by necessity she would add the words of hope to that. She knew how to do that. She had come this far, and she would not stop, she would not lose hope. Life had held very little joy for her, but it had improved and she would not stop. She would not stop.

She found what she was looking for -- several miles up the road toward Taos where the road and the Rio Grande ran alongside each other. Here, she knew, she would find rocks, cliffs, water, pinion trees and plenty of big blue New Mexico sky with white clouds. Atir Cards would get plenty of scenery and her own love of it would show through. The first pull-off area did not look good -- too many cars. She drove on and started to get worried. Too many fishermen, picnickers, and river rafters everywhere she wanted to stop. Aware that ahead around the last big curve, she had only one more chance, she held her breath but saw that even though she would not be alone, there was plenty of parking space.

She tied the easel to the backpack, put on her backpack of art supplies and headed down the path to the Rio Grande where she knew she would find rocks, water, sparkling sunlight, and pine trees. The sun felt warm on her neck and she enjoyed the fragrance of the sage brush. Two fishermen returning from the river passed her on the path, but when she arrived at the river there were no other fisherman nearby, just a family picnicking down river about a hundred feet. The water gurgled over the nearby rocks.

The rocks looked slippery and dangerous. Julie wanted to sketch the family downstream so she followed a path away from the river and the rocks and when she got to a clearing within fifty feet of where the man fished with a little boy, she set down her backpack and set up her portable easel. She could see the man watching her and figured that as soon as he saw the easel he would relax.

Capturing the light on the river, the joy of the fishermen, and the shadows of the magnificent cliffs behind them proved to be a mind-consuming effort and Julie lost track of time as her brush continuously dipped in the water, the paint, across the watercolor paper, and back again for more paint.

Just as she was ready to concentrate again on the figure of the little boy, he sat down. Julie couldn't tell what the man was saying as he bent over, but it was apparent, at least for now, the little boy was done. He appeared to be crying. Disappointed, Julie watched as the man also put down his pole, and sat down by the boy. Not to be outdone, Julie pulled out a fresh piece of paper and enamored with that scene, quickly tried to capture it before they moved again -- and they did move, picking up their poles they held hands and slowly walked back toward the rest of the family. Julie was not to miss that scene either. She quickly went to another sheet of paper and captured the scene once again with the two of them walking hand-in-hand.

Julie looked around and decided her next effort needed to include the view looking up the river, including the cliffs, the trees, and the mountain behind them, which meant she needed to sit down on the rock in back of where she stood. She sat down on the rock, admired the view, and started to shorten the easel. Ready to paint, she sat back on the rock, closed her eyes, and visualized the scene in front of her and how her paper would look after she had finished. She would spend more time on this sketch because there were no moving people to incorporate. But, in her perfect peace with her eyes closed and listening to the water, Julie didn't hear the footsteps and she was unprepared for the small voice that came so close to her, and innocently said, "Hi." Julie lost her balance and fell backward and to the side and she then instinctively put out her right hand to break the fall. Everything went dark.

When Julie woke up, she was flat on her back, staring at the sky. Where was she? What had happened? The sky came into focus and the ground underneath her became real. Her head, on the hard ground, also became real. She couldn't remember where or why she was there. Her right wrist started to hurt and she turned to look at it and knew by the stiffness and pain that life had now changed dramatically. She put her head back and remembered why she was there but she still couldn't remember what had happened. As she lay there, digesting all of this, a face appeared above her, an older woman, with short curly hair and deep concern in her eyes.

"Do you hurt anywhere?" she asked.

"My wrist is starting to hurt," said Julie.

"Would you like for me to help you sit up?" she asked.

"Sure," said Julie but quickly said felt dizzy. "Maybe not. I just need to lie here for a while," said Julie.

"That's fine. I'm right here beside you if you need anything."

Julie breathed in and out, slowly. She couldn't visualize anything and positive thinking was out, so she just breathed, that's all she could do. But she also found some words that she didn't know she had or where they came from, the voice in her pleaded, God, please help me. God help me.

"Are you feeling any better?" asked the woman with the kind eyes.

"Not really."

"Let me know if there's anything you want me to do."

"I'd like you to reach into my jacket pocket and get my cell phone out and call for help," said Julie. The woman reached into one pocket after another and found no cell phone. "Maybe it fell out and it's lying around here," she said as she looked all around Julie. No phone.

"My husband is a retired firefighter," she said. "I'll go get him. He'll know what to do. Will you be all right by yourself?"

"I'm not going anywhere. I'm afraid to move. It's starting to really hurt."

The woman put a reassuring hand on Julie's forehead and smiled. "I'll be right back."

*****

The retired firefighter looked at his handiwork, the splint on Julie's arm, and said, "That's the best I can do for now. I think I can drive you down to the hospital in Santa Fe faster than an ambulance can come get you. How about I drive your car, and then you will have it close by for whatever is next. The hospital will take x-rays, but we both know it's either broken or severely sprained."

Julie nodded. "How will you get back up here to your family, if you drive my car?"

He smiled and shook his head. "Don't worry about it," he said. "Let's get you up and walking to your car. My wife will bring your things. I'm going to lift you up, and then you lean on me. Okay?"

"Okay."

Quiet and stunned, Julie looked out the window as they made their way to Santa Fe and the hospital. The pain in her wrist was not nearly as intense as the pain in her heart, the knowing that life had changed so very fast since she had driven up the mountain only a few hours earlier.

Lying on the hospital bed, covered with a warm blanket, Julie waited for the doctor and the definitive word on her wrist, her right wrist, the wrist that helped her do everything important, especially paint and earn a living.

Two sharp knocks, voices outside the door, and the doctor entered. He smiled, introduced himself, and made a feeble joke before he got down to business." Do you want the bad news or the good news first?" asked the doctor. His shiny bald head seemed like a bright light, a light of hope to Julie.

"The good news first," she said hopefully.

"The good news is that the x-rays don't show any broken bones."

Hope blossomed immediately in Julie's chest. She forgot the pain, the doctor, the austerity of the hospital emergency room, and hoped for her work and her life and what was in balance.

But the doctor spoke again. "The bad news is that it is a sprain, and it might be broken."

"What do you mean, it might be broken? If it's broken, why don't you fix it now?"

"I understand your frustration. It's actually quite a complicated thing, the wrist." He pulled out the x-rays for her to look at. "You see here, it's difficult for the x-rays to show all the little bones in the wrist, and this one right here," he pointed with his pen, "is the scaphoid, and it's common for it to be broken and not show up on x-rays. But I'm pretty sure it's broken."

Was this doctor a masochist? "Why can't you tell for sure? Can't you take an MRI?" Her voice rose as she talked.

"I'm not going to recommend that, and you're insurance company probably wouldn't go for it."

"So, if it's likely broken, but you don't know for sure, what can be done?" Julie had a hard time keeping the panic out of her voice.

"A common treatment, and the one I recommend, is to put your right arm in a cast, from below the elbow to your hand, and keep it casted for the next few weeks. If it doesn't heal properly, we'll talk about surgery."

"A cast? Like I can't use it at all?"

"That's right. What do you do for a living?" he asked, as if it was an afterthought.

"I paint. I am a commercial artist. I paint fruits and things."

"What hand do you paint with?" he asked.

"My right hand. And I have a deadline in 4 weeks."

The doctor smiled thinly. "Sorry," he said. "We'll get you fixed up and out of here with some pain killers shortly. Do you have somebody to come get you and stay with you?"

"Stay with me? For a sprain?"

"It would be a good idea for 24 hours or overnight, anyway."

"Sure." She had no intention of having anybody stay with her, but a friend to get her home -- she needed to call Faye. Julie knew her whole world had changed, and she also knew there was no way that she could see to fix it. Her stomach drew up in a tight knot of fear.

*****

Julie leaned on Faye as Faye unlocked the door to her apartment and then they both eased in through the narrow door. Julie stepped on something and almost slipped. "Damn it, I can't even get through the door of my own apartment without almost falling."

"You can't do anything without swearing, it seems to me," Faye said as she helped Julie to the recliner. Julie settled back and closed her eyes while Faye busied herself in the kitchen, heating soup. She brought out a tray for Julie and set it beside her.

"There you are. Soup, and your pain killers. You aren't going to get addicted to the pain killers are you?"

Julie chose not to answer but instead she asked, "What was it that I almost tripped on when we came in?"

Faye went to the door and looked around. "Well," she said. "You'll want this." She picked up Julie's cell phone and held it out to her.

Julie stared at it without reaching, her initial puzzlement turning to anger. So that's what that sound had been. Just her luck the phone had fallen from her pocket before she'd even left for the mountains. Sometimes she swore life conspired against her.

Chapter Four

Collin had attended church once in a while with Jan and he believed in Jesus Christ, but all that passed into the back of his mind with Jan's untimely death.

Collin didn't see much need for church, organized religion, or pastors. He knew his argument was not original, lots of people speak against such things, and argue for tolerance, the value of being a good person, and that's pretty much where Collin's mind went. Why was anything else necessary? He himself had built a fair-sized real estate business in downtown Seattle before retiring. Now he was quite comfortable, treated people decently, had a wonderful daughter in college and looked for ways to be of service as he muddled his way into retirement. He admitted it hadn't been as easy as he had thought it would be, and adjusting to a flexible schedule with no huge purpose would take some time.

This thing with May Riley, for instance, was interesting and challenging in a detached sort of way. He missed her this quiet evening. He sat on his own back porch and remembered how just recently they had enjoyed the sunset together. But now, the doctors cared for her in the hospital and he was chartered to get the great niece and nephew out to Port Tiffany. Frustrating, but he enjoyed this kind of challenge now. He had nothing at stake in the situation, but he could hopefully be helpful to May, the doctors, and maybe the niece, and he would feel good about that. Stay detached, and enjoy the ride he said to himself as he sipped his tea, but don't get too involved. Don't let anything or anybody stop his departure for Alaska on Angel.

He would call the niece again, and hoped this time she would answer. It really was the right thing for her to come out here, however briefly, and meet her aunt and make some decisions. Collin wouldn't tell the niece about May so recently saying to him she wondered who she should leave her property to. The doctors didn't say exactly how long May would live, but surely death was imminent. The nephew wasn't answering his phone. One person at a time.

Collin picked up the phone beside him and called Julie Ashton in Santa Fe again, hoping she would answer.

"Hello?" a groggy female voice answered.

"Julie, this is Collin Matthews again." No response, but she didn't hang up.

"I'm hoping you've had time to think about my request yesterday evening. I know it's all a bit of a shock, but your aunt needs you here."

"Are you crazy? Don't you ever give up? Do you realize I have a life to lead, and right now it isn't going very well?"

"I'm sorry, Julie. It's true I know nothing about your life."

"You bet your shirt you don't. Damn it, I'm an artist, you understand? I paint for a living. I support myself as a commercial artist. I fell this morning and wrecked my right wrist, like it's all wrapped up and I can't use it for six weeks. Do you get that?? I have to think of myself."

Collin opened his mouth to speak, but nothing came out. Usually quite adept at fast-moving conversation, he now could think of nothing to say.

*****

Julie hung up the phone, closed her eyes, and waited for the group to congratulate her on being so forthright. Instead of taking on the aunt's problems, she had remained calm and had taken care of herself. She had kept her boundaries between her great aunt and her aunt's busy-body neighbor, and it felt good. She waited for their input, with her head back on the chair and her eyes closed. It wasn't a formal meeting, but several of her group had shown up to lend support. She thought, since it wasn't a formal meeting, there would be a spontaneous show of support for her. But, as she sat there with her arm in a sling across her chest, she heard nothing. She opened her eyes. Ricardo, Faye, and the other two stared at her.

"I thought I handled that well," she said.

"I'm tired of your language, Julie. Does it ever occur to you to make your point with proper language?" Ricardo had the nerve to say this, sitting in her house, at least one hole in each item of clothing. And he himself hardly a seventh grade education. She was almost sure of that. The others would be more supportive.

"Really, Julie. Your language does get tiresome, but that is beside the point for me," said Faye.

"*Well*, what is the point?"

"You really need to think about what the man is saying," said Faye. "This woman is evidently about to die, that trumps your problems. Is there really any way you can see making a quick trip of a few nights away? Two or three nights? Maybe it will help you get some clarity on your life to be away? For just a little bit?"

Claire and Cindy nodded in agreement.

"I can't believe this," said Julie. "This is supposed to be a support group. Where's the support?"

"Studies show that when a person asks for input in a situation, most of the time they are just asking to be rubber-stamped," said Ricardo.

"Will you *shut-up*?" snapped Julie. "All of you are so smart -- what about my injury? How about traveling with this?" she said as she pointed at her arm.

Ricardo dared to speak again. "It isn't as if it's your leg. One time my uncle had a broken leg and he--"

"Stop it! I don't want to hear about it. Even if I were to go, I would still need help with luggage, etc."

Faye spoke again, "There are always people to help with luggage at the airport. Just have tip money ready."

Julie couldn't believe them. Where was the support? And then Ricardo said with a broad smile, "I could go with you and help you. I can take a few days off."

"I don't think you people get it. This is a huge letdown for me. I need to get ten paintings ready for a possible new contract, and now I can't paint at all. This is a disaster. And you people haven't got a grasp of that. I'm getting lectured about my language and making a trip as if nothing has happened. Besides that, there's something else about this situation you don't know." She paused. They waited. "This aunt, she did something terrible, a long time ago. I actually don't remember what it was, something about a valuable painting." Her group seemed unimpressed.

She tried again. "Some kind of awfulness between my mother's mother and Great Aunt May about this painting, and it wasn't fair, and Aunt May did it, and if she hadn't done it, my mother's life would have been easier." Julie glanced at each of their faces and waited for a reaction.

Faye leaned forward, her face serious. "I get it Julie. I get it and I think we all do. I feel for you and this whole thing is upsetting. You've had a hard life, and now a person, who may have had something to do with your life being so hard, needs you. But I also know that sometimes God has plans for us that look terrible, and sometimes it's just best to give in to the reality and trust God. This might be the next thing for you to do, to go visit this aunt. A faith-step."

"A what?" asked Julie.

"A faith-step, where you do something that's scary, but maybe it's the right thing to do, and God is with you," said Ricardo.

"That's right," said Claire. "Don't leave out the God part."

"God doesn't give me plans, I give God the plans, and sometimes he doesn't show up to do his job!" Julie yelled at all of them.

"This is the way I see it," said Ricardo. "You need to go spend a few days with that aunt, and maybe while you're there, you'll get some great insight, like you should start painting with your toes, or maybe your left hand." He smiled at her and she hated him.

"I think you're best choice is to accept my offer and take a break from your work," he continued.

Stunned, Julie looked around the room. "Do I have any other offers?" She looked at Faye hopefully. Faye shook her head and smiled.

Claire said nothing.

"You've been under a lot of stress. Probably be a great little trip," said Cindy, always irritatingly positive.

Julie looked again at Ricardo. His clothes, the dark braid down his back and the red bandana -- Julie could handle all of that. She was an artist: she was used to people who looked different, and in Santa Fe, a melting pot of cultures, lots of people looked different, to say nothing of the tourists and how bizarre they often looked. What she didn't think she could handle was his constant criticism of her, not for a whole week. He didn't like her and she didn't like him. Was he her only hope in getting through this nightmare of a week? No. Was it possible she could go see this aunt, do the right thing, and live through it? It really might be helpful to get away for a few days. There might be some money in it for her. No, she wouldn't think that way, that wasn't right. Three nights, that would be the right thing. Ricardo could take her to the airport. She would figure the rest out. Three nights, max.

Chapter Five

Herbert Humphrey the III, or HH, as family and friends called him, looked out his window at the skyline of New York City. The brokerage statement lay on the floor, the only visible disarray in the meticulous modern home that he shared with his wife. Their daughter, a journalism student at Berkeley, kept her presence known by calling frequently to ask for money. They could have insisted she attend a closer school, but he could never stop his wife and daughter when they decided on something, and who cared now? Saving money on travel expenses was the least of his concerns. The brokerage statement revealed the margin calls, and disaster loomed ahead, like a silent freight train. The fine life they all enjoyed was about to come to a screeching halt, and he would have to admit to his wife and daughter that he had mismanaged his portfolio to a degree he never thought possible. Or, he could return to Port Tiffany and the unfinished business there. The house. Time to deal with the house.

When he and Marileta married and left Port Tiffany, they took on the world, and wanted to show all those small town people they were better than any of them. HH and Marileta didn't need his parents and their money, or to be confined to the littleness of Port Tiffany. No, they were better than that, and for years created their dream. But, at some point, and HH didn't exactly know when that was, he started gambling with stocks instead of investing and now there would be a price to pay. Hell to pay.

The phone rang. He looked at it stoically. He listened to the irritating female voice of their phone service -- "leave a message...we'll get back to you" -- and then he heard his daughter's voice. He picked it up and cordially spoke to Jenna, but she, all business, got to the point of her call.

"Dad, I've got a chance to go with a study group to Venezuela this summer, could you pull together some money for me?"

"Jenna, what does that have to do with getting your degree in journalism? You might think of getting a job." This was the crucial moment. It always was. Who would give in?

Silent only for a brief moment, and then Jenna plowed on. "Dad, this is a study group being led by professors here at school who are experts in Latin American political issues. This is crucial to my career; fits perfectly with my years of studying Spanish. You've never been stingy with me before, Dad."

He had tried, many times, but he could never stand in front of Jenna when she wanted something -- especially when she also brought in her mother to take her side. And he hated himself, for once again saying stumbling inadequate words that she easily brushed off.

When HH hung up the phone and the tortuous verbal dance with his daughter was over, she had, of course, won. It was time to go back to Port Tiffany. He would take care of business there. The house, or to be more accurate, the houses, needed his attention. He would keep the cash flowing for a while longer, borrowing, moving bills and cash. But the answer to making everything really better was in Port Tiffany, and if things went well, well then, his wife and his daughter would never know how close to financial ruin they had come.

The phone rang again. Collin Matthews. Who was *Collin Matthews?*

*****

Collin, a man of talent, discipline, and accomplishment, entered May's house with no small amount of fear. He did know how to run a business, but he didn't know much about being a good neighbor, taking care of sick people, or being a host, all of which May had brought to the forefront of his life. May, by being his neighbor and by being sick, had filled his so-called retirement. If he could shove these responsibilities off onto someone else he would. For now, he was the host -- people coming to see May needed food. The first order of business -- check out the kitchen and get some basic supplies.

He looked through May's cupboards and deduced he needed to buy coffee, eggs, bread, and some fruit. For himself he would buy steaks, but he wouldn't do that for other people -- very likely this woman from Santa Fe didn't eat meat or had some other particular food abnormality. He wouldn't cater to her. Pretty much everybody liked coffee, eggs, bread, and fruit -- or they should and he couldn't see beyond that. If she wanted more than that, she could buy more or eat out, or he would take her out. HH and his wife would be in their own house and solve their own food problems.

Collin felt good about the business reason for Julie and HH coming and his part in making it happen -- a small step in the productiveness of his new retirement and he was actually almost thrilled with that part of the situation. Making the impossible happen. His forte. He made the impossible happen in the workplace, and evidently he could do it and be of service in retirement. So be it. As soon as she and that nephew arrived, the sooner he could get back to his own plans of sailing and writing.

*****

Standing in line at the grocery store, Eva, his usual checker, saw him and managed to keep checking groceries and talk to him at the same time. "I've heard what you're doing for May, that's wonderful," she said.

The news had spread. He nodded, not wanting to say anything that would add to the fast-moving gossip in this small town, but she kept on. "You need flowers," she broadcast to him and everyone else within earshot.

"I don't think May needs flowers," he said firmly.

"No, no, no," she said. "You need flowers for her house. For the guests. It's the gracious thing to do." She pointed over to the floral department as she finished with her customer.

Collin turned his cart and headed for the floral department. He was weary of her this morning, and he hardly knew her, but if his business and May's were going to be broadcast all over Port Tiffany, then he would get the flowers. The only person actually staying in the house would be Julie Ashton, but let it be known that he, Collin Matthews, was a gracious man, a man who had not only made his mark on the world, but since he had returned to the culture of a small town, he was still a man who got things done, and he got them done graciously. Yes, he would buy the damn flowers.

*****

Collin found a vase for the flowers underneath the sink and placed his haphazard arrangement on the breakfast table. Then he did a quick cleanup of the refrigerator, put away the fresh groceries, and straightened up the guest bedroom. Eva would be proud of him.

Collin returned to the hospital just after May awakened from her nap. Her blue eyes did not look as clear, but he was pleased to see her awake. He smiled at her and showed her a single yellow rose in a tiny glass vase -- a vase from her home. She stared at the flower and then at his face. Her eyes followed him as he cleared a place for the vase on her bedside table. He pulled up a chair and put what he hoped was a comforting hand over hers.

"She's coming," he said gently. "Your niece, Julie, is coming to see you. This is what you wanted, I think, but if it doesn't seem right to you, I will know it by looking at your face. So just remember that. I know you better than she does, and if I see that something weird is going on, and I see by your face that you are unhappy, then I will pitch a fit, and stop whatever is going on." Was that the glimmer of a smile? "HH is coming, too. He and his wife were already planning to come."

Chapter Six

The day began with Ricardo driving her in the early morning from Santa Fe to the airport, and then the long airplane trip to Seattle, and then a taxi ride to the ferry terminal. Julie didn't have time to look around at the waterfront but moved briskly with the crowd to buy her ticket and then toward the turnstiles, ever careful of her healing wrist. Managing her suitcase, the ticket, the turnstile, and her cast was challenging, but with help from the man behind her, she made it on to the ferry.

Settled into a seat at the stern of the ferry, Julie gazed at the harbor, the Seattle skyline, the Space Needle, and wished for her sketchbook. It looked like a stage-setting, surreal in its grandeur. Her phone rang. Faye. "You won't believe how beautiful it is here," Julie said breathlessly. "Yeah, yeah, Ricardo was a big help, but I'm managing without him…What?… No…I can't possibly overdo because it hurts too much when I put any pressure on those fingers…I'm not sure how good the pictures will be, but I'll give it a try…Got to go, they just loaded the last cars…yeah, talk to you later."

Julie could feel the engine vibrations increase as the ferry pulled away from the dock. As best as she could she took pictures of the skyline, the harbor, and the container ships with her encumbered right hand, all the while holding on to the seat in front of her as the ferry gently rocked along. The pictures, although impersonal compared to sketches, were the best she could do. She sent the pictures to Faye and then settled back to watch the water, the wake behind the ferry, the seagulls flying overhead, screaming for a handout, and the three children at the rail, holding on, laughing, and their hair blowing in the breeze.

Julie felt at peace with herself, lost in observing this new environment, but after an hour, when people around her started getting up, collecting their things, and slowly moving toward the front of the ferry or down to their cars, Julie became uneasy again. She decided to sit still and enjoy the beauty a bit longer. When the announcement came that they were arriving in Port Tiffany, Julie got up, adjusted her rolling suitcase and silently followed the crowd.

The crowd filled the front part of the ferry. It wasn't a line, but a mass of humanity, some of them tourists, and some tired from working in Seattle -- all anxious to get off the ferry and get on to somewhere else. When the ferry docked, the gangway let down, and the gate opened. The crowd funneled through the gangway, moving gently but slowly. Julie, not wanting her arm jostled by the crowd, held back, until she was the last person to leave the boat. As she walked behind the crowd through the causeway, she felt uneasy again about what was ahead. Her career, her livelihood, her personal goals, all on the line now, and this trip to Seattle, was it going to be an expensive joke on her? The trip seemed foolish once again, but it was too late. No need to panic, because it was too late. She could only walk forward and see what happened next or what she should do next. It wouldn't last but a few days.

*****

It seemed like a thousand people walked off the ferry, to say nothing of the hundreds of cars and bicyclists that drove off the vessel. How was Collin to recognize Julie? Not by cell phone, since Collin had lost his and not bothered to replace it. Instead, he did as many others did trying to collect someone at the ferry, he wrote on a piece of cardboard, "Julie," and stood in front of those exiting the causeway. Most did not even look at him, but kept their weary heads down and marched toward taxis or cars. He peered over the heads of the waves of people, but nobody seemed to be searching for him.

Another wave of commuters exited, but no one responded to his sign. Collin waited impatiently, and as the crowd thinned, he could see one woman coming toward him. She walked slowly, her right arm in a cast and sling, and the left pulling her bag. Collin stepped forward.

*****

Julie talked little as she looked out the window and absorbed their surroundings. When Collin tried to educate her about the history of the town, she said it was too much for her on this particular day. Collin drove through the forest and into town as fast as possible without any more comment. As they entered Port Tiffany, Julie said, "It looks like any other town with all these nondescript shopping centers."

Collin said nothing, but felt his irritation level rise. As they got closer to the center of town, the character of the town revealed itself with Victorian houses and large Douglas fir trees. Julie could see the water again, the Strait of Juan de Fuca and Canada in the distance and then brick buildings of downtown and tourists everywhere. She still said nothing and Collin wondered if she missed the uniqueness of the little city totally. Santa Fe wasn't the only unique city in the country. He drove through downtown and started up the hill into another residential area, an area of more modest but still picturesque houses. As they pulled in front of May's yellow cottage, Julie leaned forward. "Wow," she said. "That's adorable. We're on a bluff, aren't we?"

"Right. Down below there's a boatyard where mostly fishermen work on their boats, and out next to the water is where the island ferry

Love that House

docks." Then he pointed to the house next to May's. "And that's where I live. Let's get you inside." He noticed she never thanked him for the ride.

*****

"It's sort of unbelievable," said Julie as she entered the house, taking in the antiques and rose motifs everywhere -- on the old wool rug, watercolor paintings of roses; even the afghan on the sofa consisted of rose granny squares. "She liked roses, didn't she?" she said as she looked at the overhead light fixture consisting of six yellow glass roses and six light bulbs. "That's unique. She liked miniatures, too. My, my, my – look at this," she said as she peered at the collection of miniature tea sets on top of the bookcase.

Collin watched her look through the kitchen, but she didn't look in the refrigerator. *Good. Criticize the roses all you want, but not my attempts to stock the fridge.* She then toured the rest of the house. When she opened the door to the middle bedroom she grimaced and said, "A quilter. Wow." She shut the door carefully and quietly as if a loud noise might dislodge the stuff that filled the bedroom.

"Hard to imagine, with the rest of the house being so neat, isn't it?" he said.

"I think some of us creative-types are that way, but that does seem over the top."

Collin placed her luggage on the bed in the back bedroom. He told her about the food in the fridge and then said, "I think it would be better if I take you to see May tomorrow morning. She's stable tonight and I know you're tired." *This day needs to be over*, he said to himself.

Julie turned to him, took her baseball cap off, unclipped her ponytail, and shook her head briefly. "That feels good," she said. He could see her tired hazel eyes, but he also saw determination.

"I want to see her tonight. I'm not going to stay here in her house without meeting her first. Even briefly."

"I'm not sure the doctor would approve," said Collin.

"I'm not going to play games with the woman. It will be brief. But it will happen."

This whole effort, this good deed, was turning out to be a pain. "Okay," he said, "why don't you make yourself at home for a few minutes. I've got a couple of chores to do next door, but I'll be right back."

In his own home, Collin stood in back of his favorite chair with his eyes closed, clutching it and leaning on it and breathing deeply. Why did this have to be so hard and why did it have to be in his life at all? He opened his eyes and looked out over the water, the ever-present and dependable water, and felt better. Yes, he would survive this and he would also be able to leave it all behind. Soon. Soon he would be on his boat and enjoying peace, sailing, and writing. But, right now he would check his phone messages. Sandy called. Left no message. He called back but she didn't answer. Okay. Time for a little nourishment. He retrieved his favorite beverage from the refrigerator, the last of a strawberry fruit smoothie. He drank out of the carton, finished it, threw the carton away, and knew he could now handle the rest of the evening.

*****

As they pulled into the hospital parking lot, Julie said, "This is really close. I could have walked."

Was she just an ungracious personality, or did the airplane ride do her in for the day? Collin chose to ignore her and moved the conversation on.

"May didn't drive a car, at least not in recent years. I can help with some transportation if you like, or we have a taxi company, and also a car rental company."

"Thanks," she said, without committing. As they walked into the hospital, Collin had the profound insight that she probably didn't like him anymore than he liked her, which was okay. He didn't feel like pandering to anybody, and that included her. For all he knew, she was a crook, a lifelong criminal. He was certainly not naïve when it came to business and people and he had a fierce loyalty to May that he took seriously. This Julie, whoever she was, would not get the best of May or him.

"You don't like me much do you?" she asked.

"Does it show?" asked Collin. "I thought I was being a perfect gentleman."

"Yes, it shows. Subtle but unmistakable. But, I don't mind so much because I don't like you either."

That made life simple. They were on the same page. They continued through the hospital without exchanging another word.

Collin opened the door to May's hospital room and as he let Julie pass through he noticed how short she was. Up until then she had seemed taller or bigger -- but that was an illusion evidently. He moved to May's bedside and Julie stood beside him.

"May. This is Julie. This is the niece in New Mexico that you wondered about, that you said you would like to get to know."

May opened her eyes. Did she actually see them? Her eyes appeared blank, but she seemed to smile at Collin, a weak smile and then she moved her hand slightly. Julie reached out and gently held her hand.

"I'm glad to meet you, Aunt May."

May looked at her briefly and then shut her eyes. It was only then that Collin noticed that Jared James had come into the room and stood beside the door. Collin motioned to each of them to go into the hall.

Collin introduced them and then said to Julie, "The doctor usually makes his rounds about 7 in the morning. I suggest I take you home and bring you back first thing in the morning."

"Absolutely not," said Julie. "I'm spending the night here in her room."

"Why would you want to do that?" he asked, knowing he sounded impatient. It had been a long day.

"Because, she's alone. Because, I don't want to go off and make myself comfortable when I won't be here that long, and I may be of use." She frowned at him. Jared James looked on with interest.

Collin asked him, "Do you need a lift anywhere?"

"No. Got my bike."

Collin handed her a card with his phone number on it. "Call me if you need anything."

He left the hospital with Jared James walking silently beside him, and knowing that he was very tired, and very tired of small town life, people and their problems, and knowing that this problem wasn't over yet. Julie Ashton wasn't anybody's answer to anything.

*****

Julie sat on the chair in the corner and watched the nurse take May's vitals and make her comfortable.

"I'm Angie, the night nurse," she said to Julie as she removed her stethoscope. "That chair turns into a bed. I can bring you a new toothbrush. Looks like you didn't come prepared for spending the night."

"That's true. I can use the toothbrush." She got up and started to pull at the bed but it didn't budge."

"Let me help with that," said Angie.

Julie looked at Angie's extended abdomen. "No, we don't need your baby to come early. I'll get it." Julie, using her good arm, put all her weight into it and the chair popped out, sending Julie to the floor.

"Are you okay?" asked Angie.

"Yes. I'm fine. There will be only one patient in this room tonight. Maybe you could make up the bed, though."

Julie went into the bathroom in May's room and sank onto the toilet, grateful for the sterile private space. She sat there with her head in her hand and listened to the quiet. She then retrieved a white washcloth from the shelf, rinsed it in warm water, and then sat back down on the toilet, with the warm cloth over her face.

Chapter Seven

Collin returned home tired and irritated with Julie, May, the doctors, and their attitudes. The situation did not have a good path and would not have a good ending. Collin didn't know the whole story about Julie's arm, but whatever it was, it certainly lessened her ability to be helpful, and that, along with her bad attitude made him wonder why she came in the first place. Maybe it was money. Maybe she came all this way because she smelled money.

The phone rang just as he entered his living room. He saw his daughter's name on the phone and settled back in his chair to talk with her. A bit of pleasantness in a long day. Hearing about her quarter finishing up and her plans for a summer job and the one class she would take this summer would be good.

The small talk went very fast and then Sandy got to the point. "Dad, I need to come home for the summer."

Home? What did she mean? Port Tiffany wasn't home for her; she wasn't raised here.

"I don't understand, Sandy. You had your plans all laid out for summer school. What are you saying?"

"I'm just not up to it, Dad. I'm all burnt out. This quarter was harder than I thought it would be. Honestly, Dad, I won't be any trouble. I'll get a job."

She wasn't telling him something. What was it?

"Are you sure this is what you want?" He could see the path, the dream he had for her, cracking and dreams needed to be pursued full force. "Do you need to talk about it?" he asked hopefully. What about his plan to sail through the Townsend Islands this summer and write his book?

"No, Dad. I just need to be with you for the summer. It's all been a lot to handle, Mom's death and school. I just need a break."

"Sandy, I had planned to sail and spend time in the islands this summer, writing the book your mother had always wanted me to write."

"Dad, if I can just stay in your house, get a job for the summer, and if you're in and out that's okay."

What was wrong? It had been almost two years since her mother had died. Maybe she was stalling out because of that, but it didn't seem likely to him. Maybe she was sick. Maybe she was pregnant.

*****

The next morning Collin drove to the hospital to check on May. He found Julie talking to the doctor in front of May's room.

"I advise you to put her in a nursing home where she will be taken care of twenty-four-seven," the doctor said.

"How long do you think she has?" asked Julie.

"Hard to tell, but I think one to two weeks."

Julie shook her head. "I can't do that."

"Can't do what?" asked Collin.

"I can't take her to a nursing home. She has only one or two weeks, and it seems to me the least I can do is take her home to die."

Aha, thought Collin. She's seen the cottage overlooking the harbor and *she's digging in. It's the money.*

Collin didn't stick around to help Julie with arrangements. The last thing he wanted to do was further entangle himself in May's family matters. He left the hospital, determined to put all this business with May and Julie out of his mind, and headed to the one place he could completely lose himself. Time to focus on his needs for a change.

Collin sat on the deck slowly moving the foam brush and the varnish over the house on his sailboat. He hardly glanced at the blue sky, the boats, or the blond sunbathing two boats away. He couldn't worry about Sandy or May or anybody else. Varnishing the woodwork on a boat was a skill, an art that he took seriously. He took it so seriously, he concentrated so much on making the brush strokes smooth over the wood that he didn't notice a person walking up to the boat until he heard a deep voice say, "Collin? Collin Matthews?"

Collin looked up, frowning, and saw a slim man in front of him on the dock. "Yes?" said Collin.

"We met the other day at May's house?"

"Sure. The pastor. Come aboard. I need to finish this varnish job before it rains tomorrow." He didn't really need a visitor.

Andy easily took the two steps in stride and bounced onto the boat. "She's beautiful, just beautiful. You must be proud."

"I am pleased. She's a lot of work. How did you know I was here?" he asked as he went back to his task.

"One of my parishioners, she kept telling me about this good-looking guy that has just moved into town and had a sailboat. And I remembered the name."

"I've hardly talked to anyone in town. I'm retired early. It's been good to just be quiet. My elderly neighbor is about the only one I've talked to much." He kept working, waiting for Andy to bring up God, church. Come to church.

"Well," said Andy as he gracefully settled down on the deck, "I won't tell you who. I also heard you lost your wife. I'm so sorry."

"Did you ever marry?" asked Collin.

"Never did."

Collin dipped his brush back in the varnish again, moved the brush over the wood, unable to say anything, while Andy closed his eyes and appeared peaceful.

After several minutes, Andy opened his eyes and spoke. "A lot of people consider the kind of work you're doing tedious, and would prefer to hire someone else to do it."

"I like doing it. I don't smoke, don't drink, but I do this."

"That's about how I feel about drawing. Actually can't do it very well, but it's a good thing for my mind to do."

"So preaching and sharing about Jesus isn't the only thing you do?" Collin knew he hadn't really delivered a question, and so did Andy. Another long silence.

"I love the Lord, and His world is big," said Andy.

Collin nodded and kept working. He could think of no smart reply.

After a while Collin couldn't bear the silence. "Are you interested in boats?"

"My dad had all of us kids sailing a little boat on a lake near our house. Haven't done much as an adult. I'd like to try some sailing now. You planning any trips?"

"Soon as I get this boat ready, I'm headed north to the islands to spend the summer sailing and writing. That was the plan before my wife died, and I'm planning to fulfill it."

"I'm a fast-learner."

"You'd have to learn more science if you're going to sail with me. Spiritual stuff won't be enough," said Collin. He couldn't resist saying that.

Andy ignored him. "There's a mother of someone I know, she lives on Bailey Island. Ever been there?"

"Anchored in the bay. Had my dog with me, and in the middle of the night the dog woke up and wouldn't stop growling. I wondered what could be upsetting him, anchored out by ourselves in the middle of the bay. But I got up, went topside, and as I stood there, looking over the water, lit by moonlight, a whale blew. Close to the boat, powerful. Then nothing. That whale must have been circling the boat and the dog knew it." Collin didn't mention how close to God he felt at that moment. "You need to go up there?" Collin liked refocusing on his trip and the islands. Get the focus off his neighbor, his daughter, and a general unease about his life.

"I need to go within a couple of weeks and check up on this woman."

How smart was Andy? Collin had little respect for the clergy of any church, and did not look forward to sailing with someone who didn't know much about it. But Andy needing to go to the islands added impetus to his trip. Those who would dissuade him would not easily argue with a pastor.

"Sure. Let's do it. Soon. I'll take you up and you can get the ferry back."

Chapter Eight

As they got out of the taxi, HH looked at the house with disdain-- big, old, like something out of an unpleasant movie. Well, soon they would be rid of it and move on. But business first. No, that wasn't true. Pandering to his wife and the neighbors was first on the agenda. They all thought he was Mr. Amiable, Mr. Local Boy Made Good, and so it must be played out. One day at a time, he would impress them all and take care of the business quietly, thoroughly, and no one would be the wiser.

"*Oh*," said Marileta as they entered the front door. "It's just like we left it, except for the dust. Lots of work to do."

HH stacked bags inside the front door and then looked around. "Let's hire someone to clean, shall we?" He said it hopefully but without confidence.

"Oh, no," said Marileta. "That wouldn't do. The neighbors would think we were showing off. Let's just get with it ourselves. It won't be hard if we get right to it."

"I'm going to call the pastor and see if he knows a kid that needs some money. Cleaning the house is not a priority for me." Work it out, one day at a time. First priority, as soon as he had privacy, call Fran in Stillwater Harbor on Bailey. The clock started with that phone call.

*****

Julie sat on May's front porch with her sketching pencil in her left hand. The woodless pencil enabled her to use the side of the pencil which created shading instead of lines. The marks looked crude, since she was using her left hand, but the side of the pencil was forgiving as a technique. No way could she make fussy little lines with this technique and she was liking it more than she thought she would. Sketching with the side of the pencil kept her looking at the lights and darks of the flowers and so she kept on, waiting for the nurse to finish bathing May. She lost herself in the beauty of the yellow roses hanging over the porch until she heard "Ahem." She looked up and saw Jared James standing not five feet away from her.

"Hard what you are trying to do," he said. "Is painting your hobby?" he asked politely.

She hated that assumption. "No, it's what puts food on the table. There's a small bone in my wrist which is likely broken. The doctors are trying to get it to heal without surgery." She was now talking like older people, steering any and all conversations to her own health issues.

"Sorry," he said as he nervously started to pace back and forth on the sidewalk. "If it isn't too much of a bother, I wonder if I could see May for a few minutes."

"It isn't a bother to me, but the nurse is busy giving her a bath right now." Julie gave him one of her stern looks, hoping he would get the hint and leave.

He turned and started to leave and then stopped and said, "May and I had an interesting tradition. I would bring by some fresh produce from the Farmer's Market on Saturday morning, and she would fix a salad for us to eat later that evening. I wondered if you might be interested in continuing that tradition."

What an odd man. "Mr. James--"

"Jared, please."

"Jared. I was under the impression that May didn't have any friends, and really, at this time of her life, I think it would be useless, considering everything."

"It's like this," he said with some urgency. "Maybe we weren't that good of friends over all these years, but we've known each other a long time and we were in the process of reconnecting with this Saturday supper thing. It was a developing tradition."

"Jared, like was this something you and she did for months or years or?"

"Okay, I'll admit, it was only the last few weeks. But we were reconnecting."

This was the most insane stupid thing Julie had heard, but maybe it had some merit.

"I hardly think May needs anything disruptive right now," said Julie. "The doctor said that she can hear, and we all need to be careful about what we say."

"I agree."

"But maybe it would be comforting for her to have you come for a visit. Will you remember what the doctor and the nurses keep telling me that hearing is the last sense to go, and to make sure what she hears is pleasant and nurturing?"

"Yes!" said Jared James hopefully.

"So, if she is still alive on Saturday, why don't you drop off the food, and I'll fix us a salad for later in the day. And let's both keep the conversation upbeat. Maybe I'll invite her nephew if he gets into town. Agreed?"

Jared's face fell. "I'd really like it if no one else is invited."

Sandy sighed. "Sure. Just you and me and May."

He smiled as if she had just given him a huge gift and returned to the bicycle he left at the curb.

"Is riding bicycles a big deal around here?" asked Julie. "No offense, but you're rather old to use a bicycle as transportation."

"My assistant manager and I get around quite well with bicycles, but you're right, it's mostly a young people's mode of transportation." He settled in on his bike, waved at her, and rode off back to the museum.

Julie continued to sketch and became increasingly frustrated with the results. So much so that she carefully took off her sling and put the pencil in her right hand. Surely this would work, using just her fingers and the cast in place. The pain took her breath away. Carefully she placed her arm back in the sling and the sling back around her neck, convinced more than ever of the necessity of following the doctor's instructions. But what was she going to do? Paintings for Atir Cards would not materialize out of this situation.

Collin Matthews drove up, gave her a cheery wave, and went into his house. Good. Glad he didn't want to talk. She didn't want to talk. Especially to someone who was always that happy. He probably had all of his ducks lined up, everything going well in his life, and she didn't want to hear about it. She couldn't imagine what she was going to do. They wanted to see more of her work and she needed a miracle. If there was a God, he certainly wasn't looking after her.

Back in the house, the nurse gone, May sleeping peacefully, Julie knew she needed a project, something she could control, something that would feel satisfying, and what came to mind was the unbearable mess of clippings, photos, and old greeting cards on the walls in the middle bedroom. She entered the bedroom with determination, but the mess on the walls stopped her cold. What should she do? The best thing to do would be to just take everything down, place it all in a large box, and then at some point go through them and possibly throw most or all of it away. Clippings, old greeting cards, post cards. There might be something of value there, but the main thing would be to get it off the walls. It was so bad she could feel the mess when she was in every other room in the house, preying on her peace of mind.

Julie picked up a box on the floor, dumped the contents on the bed, and started to unpin the first items on the wall, when her phone rang. Greg Learner from Atir Cards. She said hello while she moved outside to the front porch. He asked how she was coming along with her painting. Should she tell him the truth? Sitting down on the steps, she took a deep breath and told him where she was and what had happened to her arm.

"Julie, your life is falling apart, isn't it? I'm so sorry." That was better than she got from most people, and she took it as an opportunity.

"Greg, I still want this opportunity. I really think I could be good at this. Could I have more time?" More time, what did that mean, how much time to get her wrist healed and then produce worthwhile paintings?

"This is all unfortunate Julie, but unfortunately business is business, you understand that?"

Yes, of course she did.

"I'll still be looking at the other portfolios in the next few weeks, and likely making a decision. But, at the end of the summer, I'll be reviewing portfolios again, looking for landscape artists, with a modern technique, not super detailed, but inspiring. Maybe you could aim for that."

So, all was not lost. Just sort of. What did that mean, modern technique? Would her wrist actually be healed, and how soon could she get back home to her studio? How long was May actually going to live?

She hung up just as Collin Matthews marched across the grass and said "Hi! Beautiful day!"

"Shut up!"

Chapter Nine

Collin, a master at doing business and managing people, was not sure what to do with this middle-aged woman who wore her hair in a ponytail, who could at times be admirable, and at other times, rude. At this time in his life, when he worked to give back to whatever forces existed within the universe, God's forces that had blessed him so much, he wanted other people to respect him and his good intentions. May had appreciated him, but Julie did not and Collin didn't appreciate that. But he would not be stopped.

He planted himself in front of Julie. "I'm here to see May," he said firmly, still smarting from the unfriendly greeting. She didn't look the least apologetic for the remark, but motioned for him to go inside.

He sat down beside May and looked at her peacefully sleeping. The fan at the foot of her bed kept the air pleasantly fresh, and he noticed the flowers at her bedside. He bent over her to read the card.

Just then the voice in back of him said crisply, "They are from her church."

He sat down, feeling chastised, and then pulled *The Port Tiffany Herald*, out of his jacket pocket and unfolded it. He started to read out loud, when he felt a firm hand on his shoulder. He looked up to see Julie frowning at him and motioning him outside.

"What do you think you're doing?" she asked as they faced each other on the front porch.

"I was told that hearing is the last sense to go, and reading to her would be a good idea."

"It's a fine idea, except not the newspaper, full of weird bad news. She needs something uplifting, like maybe the Bible or something."

"You don't think the *Bible* has a lot of murder and mayhem in it? At least this newspaper is about people in her own town."

Julie went back into the house and started scanning the books in the bookcase. She picked one and then handed it to him. "This ought to be appropriate," she said.

Not wanting to create any disharmony in May's presence, Collin picked up the book and started reading *Glacier Pilots of Alaska*. He rapidly got interested in the stories, and read aloud one story after another, of the stress and challenges of flying in the Alaska wilderness. May was a very unusual woman to be interested in such a book, and he started to enjoy himself and forget about Julie.

Two of the stories had tragic endings, but Collin could tell where those were going and made up his own quick happy ending before he read them out loud to May. Julie busied herself in the kitchen.

When Collin returned home, he found Andy Harris sitting on his front porch.

"I have a question for you," Andy said cheerfully. Since Collin said nothing but sat down beside him on the step, Andy continued. "I've got a young friend, he's actually Jared James' grandson. Missing part of his left arm and having a hard time. His dad died a few years ago."

Collin shook his head at the horror of it.

"He used to help his dad on the family farm. Also helped his dad make very fine handmade chairs. He graduated from high school a year ago, but he's depressed and floundering. I wonder if you had any chores around your boat that he could do. Just to get him outside and physically working again." Andy looked hopefully at Collin, who sat very still, thinking, thinking, and thinking. Why did he retire? Life had become so complicated since he retired. People with problems, that's all he had on his plate, and worn by it all, he didn't want to take on another problem.

"I don't know, Andy. I can't fix his life. Why don't you pray or--"

"I'm not asking you to fix him. I'm asking you to help him by getting him on a boat, a sailboat, working on the wood."

"Listen, Andy, I don't let just anybody on my boat--."

"You obviously think I'm asking you to do something that would be harmful to you. You're a self-centered man."

"Is that anyway for a pastor to talk?"

"Don't try to play offended here, Collin. Why don't you come with me and I'll introduce you to this kid. Can you spare five minutes?"

"Let's go. The sooner I do what you want, the sooner I'll have my evening back to myself."

They walked down the sidewalk, past two houses, and stopped at a white picket fence. Andy pushed it open and they entered a shady yard where they saw at the corner of the porch a small young man sitting on the grass. He leaned on what remained of his left arm while he pulled weeds with his right hand.

"Heh, Tyler. This is a friend of mine, Collin Matthews," said Andy.

Tyler got up slowly, and when he turned around Collin could see that his arm below his left elbow was gone. Collin looked into the young man's blue eyes and could see the pain and defensiveness. Neither offered to shake hands.

"Tyler is doing odd jobs for people, like weeding flower beds," said Andy.

What a stupid job for a young man, thought Collin. Before he had a chance to think, the words came. "I hear you're good at varnish work."

"Not anymore," said Tyler.

"I've got my boat, my pride and joy, down in the harbor. I'm fixing her up for the summer and I could use some help," said Collin. His last holdout for privacy. What had he done?

"I don't think so," said Tyler. "I'm not interested in boats or woodwork anymore."

"Tyler used to help his dad make furniture. He knows how to varnish like a professional."

"That's exactly what I need on Angel," said Collin. "But, I need some help. Most people aren't careful enough to suit me. The varnished wood on my boat needs to be furniture quality and I pay well."

Tyler looked down at his feet and then off at the distance. Come on kid. Take a chance, thought Collin. Pulling weeds in a flower bed is no job for you.

*****

You couldn't overstate the importance of a polished well-kept cap rail on a boat, and the Honduras mahogany cap rail on Collin's boat was especially beautiful, circling the deck, framing the boat much like a woman's hair framed her face. Whether you were on the boat or walking up to it, if the cap rail looked worn and uncared for, then the whole boat looked bad and you thought less of the owner. Collin thought of these things as he stood on Angel's deck, drinking coffee, and also thinking of his own weight problem and the discomfort of getting down on his knees and working on the cap rail. He took his cup of coffee down into his boat and surveyed the needed chores. He decided to oil the purple heart chart table.

As he firmly moved the soft cloth and the oil over the table, he heard a voice coming from outside. "Hello? Hello?" Collin climbed up the ladder with labored breathing and hoped that Tyler might be there. He must lose some weight -- getting to the deck shouldn't make him out of breath. He climbed onto the deck and then stood catching his breath. Tyler stood on the dock. Good. Very good.

"Tyler, good to see you. Are you here to work? You can see, the cap rail needs attention."

Tyler nodded.

"Come aboard then."

"Here's everything for sanding, the tack cloths for cleaning. Expecting you to do a good job, finishing what you start. To look right, you've got to do all this and the varnishing in one day." Tyler nodded.

"Before you start, would you go down and get my cup of coffee? I'm going to sit here and watch how you do this."

"I don't blame you for not trusting me," said Tyler as he started down the ladder.

"I don't trust anybody when it comes to Angel," said Collin.

*****

Collin liked the way Tyler carefully started sanding the rail cap, showing skill and patience in his work.

"You're doing good sanding," said Collin. "You learned from your dad, is that right?"

Tyler didn't answer for a while. Collin thought maybe he hadn't been heard. But Tyler stood up, stretched, and then said, "I guess it was my grandpa, too."

"Your grandpa is Jared James, right?"

"Yep. We used to build model airplanes when I was little. Very delicate work, you know. He taught me to be very careful. Of course there's the dollhouse."

"What about a dollhouse?"

"My grandpa owns it. It's been in the family a long time. He keeps it in excellent shape. It's a valuable antique. It's going into the museum at some point."

"Did he let you work on it?"

"Only a little bit. He said I wasn't good enough to work on a priceless antique."

Tyler sat back down and continued to work. Collin wanted to ask him, *what happened to your arm? Are you going to get a prosthesis?* But Collin could tell that Tyler didn't want to talk, that somehow he needed to be grateful for the young man's help on this rare sunny day, and let his questions go.

As Tyler finished the sanding, Collin checked it in several places, and admired the consistently fine work. The afternoon still young, and Tyler made no mention of leaving, so Collin gave him the sponge brush and the varnish. Tyler, however, took the time to go over the wood again with the tack cloth. Then he stood up and walked to the back of the boat, and reached for the can of varnish. He lost his balance, kicked the sandpaper box over the side of the boat and he twisted back around, trying to catch it, and kicked the can of varnish. Collin lunged at the can and Tyler at the same time, barely keeping the can from going over the edge, but he also grasped Tyler's belt and managed to keep him out of the water. They sat down hard gasping for breath.

"That was close. Sorry," said Tyler. "I'm clumsy."

"Things happen fast on a boat. Go slowly, that's my motto. And always be holding onto something. Keep your balance at all times."

"Sorry about the sandpaper. Maybe you don't want me to varnish now."

They both watched the small box of sandpaper slowly move away from the dock while it filled with water.

"It's okay," said Collin. "It'll sink pretty soon."

"Maybe you don't want me to varnish?" asked Tyler again.

"Finish the job you signed up for," said Collin. "Plenty of daylight left."

Tyler didn't move, but watched the water-logged box sink out of sight.

"Did you hear me?" asked Collin.

"What?" asked Tyler.

"Get a move on," said Collin. "Get to work. You've got to finish the varnish work this afternoon. I don't want to see any varnish seams on this cap rail. Got that?"

"Yes. Yes sir."

Chapter Ten

Jared James bent over the dollhouse, looking through the chimney. The dollhouse stood in the basement of the house he shared with his daughter Karen and her son, Tyler. Over three feet tall and four feet wide, a replica of a three-story Victorian house, built by his great grandfather in the 1800s. After Jared finished looking carefully down the chimney with his flashlight, he moved to inspect the windows of the third floor. Voices and footfalls on the stairs drew his attention. He didn't need that. He quickly put the flashlight away and went to stand at the bottom of the stairs so he could intercept the intruders.

Karen descended the staircase and behind her HH laboriously took one step at a time. No, no, no.

"Look, Dad! Look who's back in town," said Karen.

"Great. How are you?" asked Jared.

Before HH could answer, Karen said, "Oh, look, you got the dollhouse out." She started to take the last step but Jared put out his arm and held onto the bannister, blocking the way.

"Karen, why don't you go fix some coffee, and HH and I will be up in a minute."

Karen looked puzzled, but didn't question her dad. She turned and left HH on the stairs.

"Long time no see," said HH. He looked over at the doll house and said, "Good you have it out. I'd like to see it up close."

"No. Not today," said Jared.

"You know; you can't avoid me forever. I know the painting's in there, you greedy, obsessive little weasel."

"Here's the thing. You're not welcome in my house. I strongly suggest you turn around and leave. Tell Karen you don't have time for coffee." Jared leaned forward as he spoke.

HH tried to stare him down but couldn't. He turned around and lumbered back up the stairs without saying a word. Jared started up the steps, anxious to hear whatever HH said to Karen in the kitchen. HH made his regrets to her about leaving so suddenly, and then Jared heard the sound of the front door as it closed.

Jared emerged into the kitchen and Karen poured him a cup of coffee. "That man is very odd," she said.

Jared didn't reply as he sipped the coffee. What was he going to do with HH?

Just then the back door slammed and Tyler slouched in. He poured himself a cup of coffee and then, without talking, planted himself in front of the TV.

"What's he been doing all day?" asked Jared.

"I don't know. He started off weeding Mary Beth's garden."

"I heard that," Tyler said from his chair. "For your information Pastor Andy got me a job with that new guy in town, Collin something. He hired me to varnish the cap rail on his sailboat."

Jared raised his eyebrows and nodded at his daughter. "Great ,Tyler. I'll bet you did a good job."

"Did you like working for him?" asked Karen.

"Yep. He's all right."

"He's taken an interest in May, he's her next door neighbor," said Jared. "I think he's a good guy."

Karen lowered her voice. "What kind of interest? Maybe he's after her money?"

Jared replied, "I don't think so. He has plenty of his own, I think. He's made sure her niece and HH are stepping up to their responsibilities at this time. I'm going to have dinner with the niece and May Saturday night."

*****

Hard, nerve-wracking work, watching Tyler sand and varnish the cap rail. Actually it would've probably been easier if he had done it himself. As Collin contemplated that, he also contemplated the steps in front of him, the steps up the bluff to his house. Committed to climb them every day for the exercise instead of driving, he squared his shoulders and began, ten steps at a time, rest, ten more, rest, and so he made it to the top, not dangerously out of breath. He crossed the street and approached his own back door, but he saw the car parked in his driveway. Sandy's car. She opened the door for him. "Hi, Dad."

*****

Saturday morning Jared placed his favorite basket, the one he used for the farmer's market, on his bicycle and took off for the market, where he selected the vegetables and smoked salmon he wanted for dinner that night. He started slowly down the hill to May's house. The breeze felt good on his face, the smell of the salt air, and the ships passing in the Strait -- he loved living in Port Tiffany.

When he swung in to the driveway at May's house, he saw Julie, standing in front of her easel on May's lawn, with a blue bowl of rhododendrons on a table. She held a palette knife in her left hand and her eyes fixated on the blank canvas.

"Are you fearful of making the first marks on that beautiful white canvas?" he asked.

"Yes! I'm petrified."

"How many years have you been doing this?" he asked.

"A long time, but I never get over my fear of the blank canvas. And this time I'm using my left hand."

He did the only thing he could do. He took the palette knife from her, already loaded with blue paint, and pushed it across the canvas. In one slow stroke he left an uninterrupted beautiful line of paint. Then he handed the knife back to her and stood there smiling.

She looked at the canvas and then at him, and said nothing. Probably shouldn't have done that, he thought, knowing that he had likely just ruined an expensive canvas. She might never forgive him. Why oh why did he have to do that?

But just then, she started to giggle, just a little giggle, but it made Jared relax. And before either of them knew what was happening, she loaded her palette knife and made her own colorful mark across the canvas.

As she added more strokes with her palette knife, he admired her work and then asked if he could put the produce for their dinner that night in her kitchen. She nodded, intently focused on her painting. He picked up the basket on his bike and quietly entered the house. May slept peacefully. Soft music played on the radio, and the sound of the fan made the room pleasant. All was well. Everything being done in a timely manner. He found himself breathing more easily as he finished his chores in May's house, said goodbye to Julie, and left.

*****

Painting with a palette knife in her left hand, Julie found it impossible to attempt any detail. She painted with color and large shapes trying to capture the blue sky and the rhododendrons in front of her. After painting through the morning, she fixed lunch for herself, and then spent the afternoon on another canvas, checking throughout the day on May, who slept on in a world only she knew. Filled with excitement but tired, she reluctantly put her painting materials on a corner of the porch and went into the kitchen to prepare the salad she and Jared would share for dinner.

Julie set the table in the kitchen, and then sat down beside May to wait for Jared. At 5:15 he hadn't arrived, but she wasn't worried. By 5:30 she'd grown concerned but not enough to interrupt her reading of a magazine. By 5:45, however, she paced around the house, looking through all the windows. Where was he? He didn't strike her as a man who would be casual about commitments. Hadn't he wanted this dinner and planned it? So, where was he?

She checked on May again, fixed her blankets and turned off the music for the night, when she heard a loud knock on the front door. Julie opened the door to see Collin trying to catch his breath and Jared James nowhere in sight.

"I know you're expecting Jared," he said, "but he's not coming."

"Why not? What happened?"

"He's dead," said Collin.

Chapter Eleven

Julie sat on May's front porch and tried to absorb how life had once again changed unexpectedly and without reason.

"What happened? You said a bicycle accident? Did a car hit him?"

Collin sat beside her with his head in his hands. "No. He rode his bike down the path from the upper bluff, where he lives, and his brakes failed. It gets real steep there, and he crashed. Someone saw it, called for help, called Karen, and she called me."

"I don't understand," said Julie.

"It can happen. Brakes can fail. I have to think that he's made the trip on his bicycle a thousand times, but brakes can fail and then create a disaster."

"He wanted to be here for dinner." Julie could hear her voice rising, almost to a screech. "It was his idea, and he brought by the makings for dinner this morning. It wasn't my idea, it was his. And now he's dead and May is still alive, and I don't know why I care. I'm real concerned about my career, and all I can see is a mess. A mess interfering with my life, and no way out."

"I'm going over there right now. See if I can help. Neighborly thing."

She said nothing, staring out into space. He left to once again do the neighborly small-town thing, but he had no idea what he would say to Karen or Tyler.

The morning of Jared James' funeral, Collin stopped briefly at the kitchen door. Sandy looked like her mother, sitting at the kitchen table in a fluffy blue robe working a crossword puzzle.

"Hi, Dad. You want me to make you some breakfast?"

"No, thanks. I'll get some cereal and coffee."

He sat down next to her with his food. She put her pencil behind her ear just like Jan did. Collin looked away and started on his cereal.

"Do you know a word for melanin?" she asked.

"No. Too early for me to work my brain that hard. Seems like somebody who was interested in being a doctor would know that word."

"Dad. Please don't take potshots at me."

Could they ever just have a simple conversation?

"What are you going to do today while I go to the funeral?" he asked

"I thought I would read some. It seems like I haven't been able to sit down and read a book for ages. And maybe go see your next door neighbor and see if she needs any help with her aunt. Aunt May she calls her."

"Mmm," said Collin

He took his mug to the sink and started to rinse it out.

"I'll do that, Dad."

"I don't need to be waited on, Sandy." He turned and looked at her and then looked away. She looked hurt. He didn't need to do that. But disappointment in her grew by the hour.

"You know, Dad, I don't want to be in your way. I'll find a job soon."

"It's all going to be fine," he mumbled. "I've got to go work on my boat. I'll come back to change my clothes for the memorial service."

"Sure."

*****

Collin sat in the back of the crowded church. He made an attempt to sing, listened to Andy talk about Jesus Christ, listened to the mayor expound on the life of Jared James, mainly his long association with the museum. After the last prayer, Collin moved through the crowd toward the side exit when Andy stopped him.

"Jared's daughter, Karen, asked me to ask you to come by the house for lunch," said Andy.

"Why me? I hardly knew the man," said Collin.

"She found out what you did for Tyler."

"You mean having him come work on my boat? That's hardly a big deal."

"Please, Collin, just come. You'll meet more of the townspeople and it's her way of saying thank you."

*****

The cottages of Collin, May, and others perched on the small bluff above the boatyard, giving the owners a short walk to the island ferry, boats, and some shopping. The bigger bluff to the east held the larger houses -- mostly three-story Victorians, one of which was HH and Marileta's, handed down from his parents. Jared James' house, located on the water side of the street, looked entirely different with one story and a basement. The brick exterior and ranch style hugged the edge of the bluff, not looking modern or Victorian. Karen, Jared's daughter, stood at the door greeting people as they entered her home. Collin waited, hoping no one could tell how impatient he was, and how much he wished he had gone to his boat with a sandwich. Finally, she turned to him, her clear blue eyes sad but she smiled warmly.

"Thank you for your efforts toward my son, Tyler," she said. If anything made him nervous, it was talking about another man with his mother.

"Just business. He has some skills I'm paying for."

"I hope he does good work. His dad and his grandpa certainly

Love that House

worked with him a lot."

He still didn't want to talk about Tyler but politely said, "If I wasn't happy, I would have told him."

She smiled uncertainly while she turned to the people behind her. Collin maneuvered through pockets of people in the living room and into the dining room where he perused the buffet and where he found Julie, pouring coffee.

"What are you doing here?" he asked. "I thought you could hardly leave the house. I thought you didn't know anybody."

"Your daughter made it possible. She needed a job today and I needed to get out. Wasn't hard to pick up the phone and volunteer to help. He was, after all, very important to May. But, having said that, I'm glad to pour coffee and listen to the local chitchat."

He stood behind her, drinking his coffee, and listening to how adeptly she talked with the people, something his wife had been very good at. They all wanted to share a memory or a story about Jared James, and nobody seemed to be grieving. The good food and the good memories flowed.

*****

"Julie, I'd like you to meet one of our small town boys made it big, this is Hubert Humphrey, III or HH as we call him, and his wife Marileta. They just happened to be visiting from New York," said Karen.

"Good for us to meet," said Julie. "We have the same relationship with May, which makes us related, distant cousins." They awkwardly shook hands, and then Marileta immediately and breathlessly started talking.

"I hear you're an artist. How wonderful to support yourself with painting. That's unusual," said Marileta.

"Yes, and difficult with a sprained possibly broken wrist. But, I am starting to love this town and the history in it. I understand your families have long-time roots here," said Julie.

"Yes," said HH. "May's family and ours and Jared's go back a long ways, back into the mid-1800s. Our house, the big Victorian down the street, dates from 1890. And of course we have a long association with May."

"I've noticed that house. It's lovely. I'd like to try painting it if you don't mind," said Julie.

"Of course we wouldn't. Maybe you would like to see the inside?" Marileta asked. "Even though I married into the family, I love the old house. It's the biggest and oldest in town and I'm proud of it."

"You're probably very busy, taking care of Great Aunt May. And we appreciate you doing that," said HH before Julie could respond to his wife. "I would offer our help, but it looks like you have it under control, and it won't last long."

Sure, thought Julie. I'll bet once she dies, you make your presence known in my life more than I want. Just stay away. I know what to do, how to care for a helpless human being.

*****

Collin wandered through the crowd of people with his coffee and a plate of tiny sandwiches. The crowd and the noise now bored him, so when he looked out the window and saw Tyler sitting in the back yard on a swing, looking lonely and sad, Collin knew he had a destination.

When he got outside, Collin put his coffee on a small table by the swing and started to eat one of his sandwiches. Tyler glanced up at him and said nothing.

"Would you like to have one of my sandwiches?" Collin asked Tyler. Tyler shook his head and kept swinging. He did not ask Collin to sit down.

"It was a terrible day for me when my grandpa died," said Collin.

Tyler did not respond.

"I know how it feels," said Collin, trying again.

"Oh, come on. NO you don't! How dare you say that! You don't know how I feel."

Collin kept eating his sandwich.

"It was a bad accident and terribly unexpected," said Karen, quietly standing beside Collin.

Tyler stood up and faced them, his face red with anger. "It wasn't an accident. How could it be? He went down the hill a zillion times, even recently!"

Tyler left, with his mother crying and Collin not knowing what to say.

"I don't know what to do with him. I know he loved his grandpa, but I can't seem to help him get on with his life."

"What did he mean, it wasn't an accident?" asked Collin.

"I don't know, but I don't care either. I love him, but I am tired of trying to fix his life, and what he means by this. I don't care."

Karen dissolved into more tears and left him, passing Andy as he entered the backyard.

Andy watched her go and then turned to Collin.

"I can't wait to get out of here. I've had enough of this town, the people, and its problems," said Collin.

"So, you're going to sail north, write your book, and avoid life, is that it?" asked Andy.

"Don't talk to me about avoiding life, look at you. You avoided life by doing what you do. That's the ultimate life avoidance. Hiding behind God and avoiding real commitments."

"Maybe so," said Andy. "But I'm staying. I see the need for help around here and I'm not leaving. This town, right now, is full of need, spiritual and otherwise, and I am here to help. You're the one leaving because it's too hard."

"You don't understand. I need to get away and write this book. It will be a tribute to my wife and the editor wants to see it by the end of summer."

"I understand that," said Andy. "And I don't know whether you should go or stay. But what I've learned in life is I go where God needs me, and I leave all the tributes to him."

Collin glared at Andy and then turned to go. He couldn't get away fast enough.

"Are you leaving?" asked Andy. "Van Crampton, assistant manager of the museum, said he wanted to meet you."

Collin turned back to Andy, his face close to Andy's and said, "I don't want to meet him or anybody else today." Once again he walked away.

Andy's voice followed him. "Can I still have a ride up to Stillwater Harbor?"

Collin waved his arm without turning around and said, "Leaving in a couple of days. Be ready or be left behind."

*****

HH watched them from the patio and then hurried into the house to find Karen. Karen, balancing a tray of sandwiches and trying to get through a crowd of people, could not make her way through to put the tray on a coffee table.

HH deftly picked up the tray and then said loudly, "Coming through!"

"Thanks, that was easy when you're big! Sorry, I didn't mean--."

"That's okay. No secret I could lose some weight. I'd be glad to help you in any way I can with Jared's affairs. Some of these things can be quite complicated." He set the tray down with a flourish.

"Thanks, HH, but actually Andy is going to help. He wants to sail to Stillwater Harbor with Collin -- that may be imminent and last for a few days, but he won't be gone long. There's a sick woman up there that Andy is concerned about."

HH watched Karen turn to talk with the elderly couple from next door, grabbed three sandwiches, and while he ate he exited through the front door and out onto the front lawn. He finished off the last sandwich and then called Fran.

"There's a boat coming up there, sailboat, named Angel, with two guys on it, and you need to make friends with the one named Andy. Somebody's sick up there, and Andy's there to check on her." He listened to her and then said, "Find out if they know anything about paintings, specifically miniatures, and specifically Bierstadt's work." He listened again, and then said, "No, you listen to me. I know, I know, it's in that dollhouse, but I don't know what Van knows, or this new guy Collin. He thinks he's pretty smart. But May wasn't-- May was stupid. But that preacher, Andy, he might know something."

HH ended the call, thought briefly about going home and letting Marileta continue the chitchat fest, but then the idea of another sandwich appealed to him. He went back in the house to find one.

Chapter Twelve

Collin stuffed the last pair of socks into his bag, looked around his bedroom, turned out the light, and decided to not awaken Sandy. She could go down to the dock if she wanted to say goodbye. He stepped into the kitchen, expecting peace and quiet, but Sandy sat there in her robe, looking out the window.

"You scared me," he said. "I thought you would be asleep."

"I think a lot more things, like whales and ships and bears are about to scare you worse," she said without turning around.

"Are you coming down to the boat to say goodbye?" he asked.

"Dad, are you sure you need to go?"

When would everyone stop questioning him about the need for this trip? He sat down in the chair next to her, and knew, when he did it, that the big sigh he let out was a mistake, but he couldn't help it.

"Yes. You'll be fine. I need to go."

He could tell by her profile that she was about to cry. He would be patient. That's what fathers do, exhibit patience. "Is there anything you want to talk about?" There. Not just patience, but a willingness to talk.

"Sometimes I miss Mom terribly," she said.

"I do too. But we have our lives to live, and she would want that. She would want me to get sailing and writing."

"And for me to go back to school?"

"I didn't say that."

"But it is what you meant."

"Look, Sandy. If you need to be here for the summer, to take a break, that's fine. I need to let you make your own decisions and I need to make mine."

She turned her head so he could no longer see her face.

"Are we square? Are we okay?" he asked.

She nodded without saying anything.

He walked through the kitchen and let the door slam behind him. He couldn't wait to get away, to be out on the water, and put distance between himself and all these people. Even his own daughter had an unnerving way of not understanding him, not understanding what life was about.

"Collin!"

Couldn't he get out of town without one more person needing him? Julie sat on May's back porch. He waited for her to speak, but he would not go over there and get hooked -- caught, in more people neediness.

"Collin, thanks for getting me square with the court so that I can run this household with May's money. Very nice that HH is okay with it."

Nodding, he said, "You're welcome." Now, could he go?

"I'm sure we can work everything out. He seems pleasant. I see no problems. Andy's been helpful, too."

Wonderful. The pastor is helpful in the business-side of life? Collin doubted it. He waved and kept walking. He walked briskly down the steps to the boatyard, through the boatyard and out on to the docks toward Angel. Tyler, May, Julie, and his own daughter -- he felt their claims on his soul loosening with every step.

*****

Collin leaned down into the cabin. "You about ready down there?" he asked Andy.

"Yep, just about. Depth sounder's working."

"How about the radar?"

"Yep."

"Auto pilot?"

"Give me a minute on that."

Collin walked back around the deck, checking the rigging of every sail and both anchors. Sandy and Tyler stood on the deck ready to cast off lines. Each having given up part of their busy day to wander down and say goodbye -- they met for the first time. Collin couldn't help but notice how well they got along, bantering with each other as if they had known each other for years. She was one year older than Tyler and certainly more mature than Tyler, but Collin didn't miss their affinity for each other and he didn't like it. He didn't like the way Tyler slumped around with the hoodie over his head. What was that about? Why didn't he get over the accident, or whatever happened to his arm, and get going in life?

"You ready down there?" Collin yelled at Andy again.

Andy bounded up the steps, smiling. Pastors It's a lot better than morose with a hoodie pulled over your head, but not by much, thought Collin.

Collin started the diesel, and enjoyed the deep sound of the engine. Andy climbed over the house to the mast and checked the rigging.

"Ready?" Andy asked Collin.

"Ready!"

"Let'er go!" Andy said to Sandy and Tyler.

Sandy, standing near the bow, untied the rope and threw it to Andy. "Have a good trip!" she said. Tyler, at the stern, did the same with his rope and the boat gently moved away from the dock. Collin didn't like looking down at the dock and seeing Sandy and Tyler getting along so well, but he quickly returned to focusing on getting the boat safely away from the other boats and heading out of the marina.

Sea gulls flapped overhead, the sun felt good on his face, and the

Love that House

sound of the diesel gave Collin a sense of joy and security. This was heaven. In a few minutes they would put up the sails. Better than heaven.

*****

"He can hardly wait to get out of the marina and put up the sails -- I can tell," said Sandy.

"What are you going to do the rest of the day?" asked Tyler as they watched Angel move through the marina.

"Help our neighbor out. Look for a job."

"Maybe your neighbor has some yard work for me?" asked Tyler

"Let's go see," said Sandy. "Let's go now. I don't want to stand here and watch until they're out of sight."

*****

The morning clicked. Without any planning on Julie's part, it clicked and the beauty of it all astounded her. Tyler, with his one and a half arms, hauled her painting supplies down the hill and set up her easel in the boat yard, facing an old wooden boat. She stood painting below May's house, using her left arm, up close to the boats. The shapes of the boats in the yard, their colors varying from white to blue to red and brown, and the blue sky and shifting clouds added to her morning, encouraging her to paint swiftly, to catch the quickly changing light. And she did paint swiftly, using small boards, almost miniatures. Julie lost herself in painting for three hours, knowing that Sandy, as she cleaned the house, kept watch over May and Tyler was working in the yard, but her concentration was broken by a gruff voice close at hand.

"Heh!"

The voice surprised Julie and she jumped. She could hardly see the man's eyes, between his heavy beard and the cap pulled down low.

"We're going to start sanding that boat." He pointed to her left. "You might not want to be here."

"Sure. Thanks for the warning." Time to go. Time to call Tyler to get all her stuff back up to May's house.

*****

Julie stacked her painting supplies in the corner of the living room and then pulled the five small paintings out of the storage container and placed them one by one across the mantel and two on the sideboard. She stepped back and admired her work. Encouraged by her own work, she felt joyful. When she didn't focus on her career and what Greg at Atir Cards might think of her work, she felt optimism growing inside herself.

She admired the clear colors and the simple shapes that came from using her left hand. Who knew if anyone else would like them -- but she did.

Julie sat down beside May and took one of the frail hands in hers. The doctor said she was going downhill, but no one knew with certainty when she would die. What would it feel like, to be this old, this close to death, and have no children to care about you? What would it feel like to have out-lived your friends at church, and have no one remember you or care? What, exactly, did May think about, lying there? Julie readjusted the blankets around May and then decided to brush May's hair.

The wispy soft gray hairs framed May's face in an angelic way; the brush barely touched them, smoothing over them. Maybe she'll surprise us all and live to be a hundred, thought Julie.

Her thoughts turned to herself. Her life on hold, with her arm in a sling, missing her appointment with Atir Cards, caretaker of a woman she didn't know but felt strangely protective of -- she couldn't imagine life being any weirder. The freedom she felt astounded her, however, and some of the things Andy said were making sense, like not focusing on the church of her past, but on Jesus and talking with him daily. Reading the Bible she found on May's bookcase. "What a friend we have in Jesus," the old song said, and the joy in that, growing slowly, pleased her so much she didn't want to talk about it. Even with Andy.

She couldn't take care of or worry about her future. She could only live one day at a time, taking care of responsibilities right in front of her. If her apartment and her career all burned up, one way or another, well, there was nothing she could do about it. Committed to being in Port Tiffany, her days full, she wondered about God and there was no one to argue with her. There were periods in her life when she had adamantly said God didn't exist and times when she ardently believed in church, but now, it was different. She couldn't do anything but believe in Jesus, and she hoped he would take care of what she couldn't take care of, which seemed pretty much like everything.

Restless, Julie got up, determined once again to do something productive with the mess in the middle bedroom. She looked at the mess on the walls and just couldn't face it, so she shut the door and went back to the living room where her eyes settled on the glassed-in bookcase. She opened the door and peered in at the faded book covers. Classics. She couldn't get interested in *Jane Eyre, Little Women* or the others. Then her eyes settled on the small desk in the corner of the living room. The top dropped down to write on, a secretary -- that's what they're called. Julie studied it briefly and then reached up to pull down the top. Locked. Then she tried the three drawers. Locked.

This wasn't right, was it? That she should be snooping through her great aunt's things. But. Her aunt lay dying. Julie, being the caretaker, needed to get into the desk. What could it hurt? Indeed, it might help.

Help her to be a better caretaker, to know what was in the desk. What if May had huge bills to be paid -- then it was righteous that Julie know about these bills. Pronto. Now. Bank accounts, information besides what Julie got out of May's purse. All right. Having convinced herself, she searched for the key earnestly.

She felt around the top of the secretary and found nothing. She felt around the top of the bookcase and found nothing. From there she tried every nook and corner of the living room but found no key of any sort. The next thing to try would be something sharp and pointed from the kitchen. Julie searched through the kitchen drawers and came up with a skewer from some long-past barbeque.

Julie poked the skewer in the hole and wiggled it gently. She tried again. Pushing gently against a mechanism she could feel with the skewer, she could feel it click but the desk top did not open. What about May's purse? What about her bedroom? In a small china bowl painted with roses on May's bedside table, Julie found a small key. The key.

Inside the desk, Julie picked up a savings account book -- not much money, if indeed the account was still open; three different packages of old letters, each bound with a rubber band; neatly organized desk supplies; and a collection of postage stamps from long ago -- some marked with $.24. In the top two drawers Julie found several small diaries, some with locks and some with no locks. Diaries, which could be interesting, but not now. She shut the drawers, picked up the savings account book and had just settled into the sofa to look through it when May started to choke and cough.

Julie quickly moved to May's bedside and turned her so that May could breathe better. Julie rubbed her back and swabbed May's mouth with water when someone knocked on the back door and then opened it.

"Julie? It's Sandy. Am I interrupting?"

"Come on in. We've had a bit of an upset but she feels better now."

Julie fixed May's pillow and straightened her blankets as Sandy looked on.

"You look a little down," said Julie. "What's on your mind?" Sandy stood, twirling her hair with one finger. Julie moved to the couch and motioned for Sandy to join her. Sandy hesitated, and then perched on the edge of the couch while she talked.

"It's my dad. He's gone on his sailing trip, coming back who knows when. I had big hopes that he and I could connect this summer, but, he's run away. Again."

Images of the desk and the still locked drawers filled Julie's mind. She did not want to be diverted from her tasks with May, but she prayed silently the simple prayer the local pastor had mentioned to her -- Lord, help me.

She heard herself saying, "Sandy, why don't you have dinner with me and maybe you would like to talk about it?" Julie couldn't believe she said that -- being that gracious and considerate of someone else was not normal for her. But, she did have a soft spot for women trying to make it on their own. And that included old women who shouldn't die alone and young women trying to figure out their path in life.

"Are you asking me to come back and share my life story with you, and all my feelings? If you are, that seems tiresome for you," said Sandy.

"I'm asking you to come back, eat dinner with me so that I'm not lonely, and I'll share some of my life with you and if you want, you'll share some with me, and maybe that's good enough. I'm not smart enough to analyze your life or give you any advice."

Chapter Thirteen

HH, looking in the hall mirror, lightly ran his hand over his hair and admired it. Most men his age didn't have as much hair, and even though the gray dominated the color, the amount of hair and his hairline helped make him unusually handsome. For his age, of course. He unbuttoned his polo shirt and smoothed the collar.

"Darling?" Marileta called from the kitchen.

HH thought of pretending he didn't hear her, but she appeared behind him and said, "Did you want to wait? I could go with you. I rather liked her and she might like it if I come with you."

"No, dear. I need to go now. She's expecting just me. Maybe another time. Another time it will be perfect."

Marileta knitted her eyebrows together in that way she had, but HH decided to ignore it. He needed to have a very important conversation with Karen, and nobody, even his wife, would get in the way.

He closed the front door gently behind him. Marileta, perfectly capable of opening the door and marching right after him if he wavered one bit, stayed behind the closed door. HH did not waver because he knew he had enough charm and smarts on his own to accomplish the task.

*****

As Karen opened the door HH arranged a pleasant smile on his face. They exchanged meaningless pleasantries as they settled into chairs in the living room. HH didn't know it would be this easy. With perfect timing he said, "I'd like to help you in any way I can, and I know we talked before, and you said Pastor Andy would likely be helping you, but I have something specific in mind."

"You're very kind," she said as she looked beyond him. Tyler stood there staring at his mother. "I think we have everything under control."

Excellent. She was ignorant. This would be easier than he thought.

"What I was thinking about was determining the value of any antiques since collecting antiques and art has been a longtime hobby of mine." He smiled broadly.

Tyler cleared his throat. "Mom, could I see you for a minute? Sorry for the interruption."

HH sat very still and waited patiently, trying to hear what they said. Karen returned with an apologetic smile.

"HH, you're such a dear to volunteer, but Dad had always said that Van should be the one to help us out with things like the antiques and art. As you know, he worked for Dad for a long time. We'll be contacting Van. I hope you understand. We wouldn't want any ill feelings between Van and us."

"Absolutely. Of course." He rose with as humble an attitude as he could maintain. Once out the door and walking down the sidewalk, he pulled out his phone, dialed with one stab, and said, "Worked perfectly." He replaced the phone in his pocket and started to whistle as he walked.

*****

Collin sat down on the deck with a cup of coffee and enjoyed the sea air and the silence that encompasses a sailboat slicing through the water. Andy skillfully kept the boat on course. Not bad for a clergyman. Collin liked the way Andy never ventured an opinion without being asked and he intuitively watched the wind, water, and ships on the strait all at the same time. Neither the autopilot nor the radar were needed. Sailing with a minimum of electronics -- Collin liked this day.

A whale blew off the starboard and Collin pointed at it; Andy nodded.

More of this, thought Collin. This is what I need. I don't need more needy people, but more of this -- the water, the sky, the birds. Andy sailed better than he had expected, but once he let Andy off in Stillwater, then everything would be perfect -- sailing, writing, fishing, all the way to Kingly Island. Meeting a few interesting people along the way where he fueled but otherwise staying alone -- his boat would be an island. Grateful he could leave Sandy behind to get her life in order. She disappointed him when she changed her mind about medical school earlier in the year and wanted to study art history, but it was her life and he had gone along with her decision. He personally had little use for art history. Sandy didn't have his drive, but very few people did.

May would die soon, likely within days. He enjoyed thinking about the brief time they shared, coffee on the back porch, her refined talk about issues of the day. An unusual woman who had no children, outlived her friends, and talked in a pleasant way, not dominating the conversation or going on and on about the weather. Too bad that situation deteriorated into neediness and messiness. How could May, someone so refined and orderly and logical, have gotten to a place in life, the end of life, with such messiness, neglecting the obvious business until it was too late? But, as he often did, he picked up the messiness and clarified it as much as possible. Now others needed to pick up their responsibilities and leave him free to his summer. And some distance between him and Julie, he needed that, too. He liked thinking about her eyes as she earnestly studied the flowers she contemplated painting, but he didn't need a woman in his life. Her career, her healing wrist, her life back in New Mexico, her relationship with HH and May -- not his business.

A container ship, longer than two football fields, bore down on them, heading out to sea. Collin watched the ship with interest and thought it a good test of Andy's sailing abilities. Would Andy turn toward the ship, expecting to go behind it, or would Andy think it was so far off and moving so slowly that he could cross in front of it? Andy turned Angel to go behind the container ship as it approached. *Good choice. Preacher isn't preaching at me and he just made a crucial big decision that not everybody could make.*

Despite the distance, the ship approached rapidly, and its size dwarfed and humbled Andy and Collin. It plowed past them, the relentless wake sending the sailboat into a bucking action.

"Turn her into the wake!" said Collin.

The sails lost the wind as Andy turned to move directly into the wake. Collin put down his coffee and scrambled to his feet to adjust the mainsail.

The ship passed and Angel slowly stabilized into a gentle rocking.

"Any tips on how I could have handled that better?" asked Andy.

"Next time, be prepared for the wake sooner," said Collin.

"Yeah. Right. Amazing how far away that thing looked but how fast it came upon us. Put some hair on my chest."

"Is that a way for a preacher to talk?" asked Collin.

As they moved into the channel between the first two islands, Collin took the tiller and Andy sat beneath the boom on the house.

"You want something to eat?" asked Andy. "I can make an omelet."

Was there no end to this man's politeness and skills? "Why don't you wait on food, I'll need some help with the sails in a couple of minutes." First he needed to adjust the trajectory of the boat, just a bit, but still keep the sail full. Success.

Angel leaned more but plowed ahead. Then the wind changed, and suddenly the mainsail, instead of full and powerful, fell in on itself, whipping loudly, and the boom hesitated only a second before it swung back -- Andy flattened himself as the boom slammed over his head to the other side and with a loud bang, came to a standstill, the boat shuddering, the sail filling, and Andy and Collin breathless, and unable to talk. Andy remained horizontal, frozen with fear.

"Heh! Are you okay?" asked Collin.

Andy slowly sat up, looked back at Collin, and nodded. "What the hell happened?" he asked.

"Accidental jibe. Scary!"

"I'll say. You could have been trying to pick me up out of the water. Glad that's over."

Collins' relief gave way to dismay when he looked at the boom. The end of the heavy wooden boom broken, hung by the sail track. "Damn. Andy, look out!"

The sail flapped loudly in the wind -- Collin and Andy grappled to tame it and bring it down and as they did the boat slowed and righted herself. The sail lay a mess of canvas over the deck, providing challenges to their safety as they then pulled the broken boom back over the house to secure it.

Collin, breathing heavily, surveyed the mess and knew they couldn't stop. He started pulling the heavy unmanageable canvas over on top of the boom and Andy followed his lead. Together they pulled and folded the sail, until layer upon layer the sail lay upon the boom where they tied it down.

"That's a mess," said Collin as he surveyed the broken boom and the untidy sail piled upon it. "I think you said something about providing an omelet before this happened. I'd rather had the omelet."

Andy nodded. "My omelets aren't a surprise. Always good. None of my omelets ever tried to take my head off."

*****

The diesel steadily growled, pushing Angel between the islands, ever closer to Stillwater Harbor. Andy and Collin, grateful for calm waters and the dependable engine, said nothing, watching the scenery from where they sat in the cockpit. A motorboat zipped by them going the opposite direction.

"That was stupid of me. I misjudged the wind pressure on the sail," said Collin.

"Pretty scary," said Andy.

"That's putting it mildly. I could have put both of us in the water with any more force on that boom. It could have been a disaster."

"True, but we are strong. We are he-men, and the boat is upright, heading to harbor, and God has blessed us."

Collin didn't say anything, but kept his eyes on the state ferry ahead. Capable of carrying 200 cars, the ferry wasn't something with which he wished to tangle. He knew he could not misjudge anything about the ferry, its speed, which way it was moving, or anything else because his boat was now vulnerable, due to his own mismanagement. He would analyze the whole incident later. He would grind on it until the total truth revealed itself. Lucky for him Andy focused on the scenery around him instead of playing a blame game. Collin blamed himself enough for the two of them.

"Hard to tell from here, but I think that ferry will turn into the harbor ahead of you," said Andy.

"I think you're right. There are so many around here, and I don't have a chart in front of me, but let's slow down and watch. No need to rush."

"No. Wow. We're both wrong. She's bypassing Stillwater and

coming our way."

"You and I better get tied up at the dock before we make another mistake," said Collin.

*****

"You've got to be kidding me," said Collin as he looked at the harbor master, a young man who Collin supposed didn't know much about anything.

"No, I'm not."

"You're telling me that all the slips are taken or reserved except for the one next to the ferry dock?"

"That's right."

"That'll wake me up all night. To say nothing of interfering with work on the boat during the day."

The kid stared him down.

"I'll take it -- but you'll let me know if another one becomes available?"

"Sure," said the kid.

Collin returned to the fuel dock where Andy finished fueling Angel.

"Get a good slip? Where are we headed?" asked Andy.

Pointing toward the docked island ferry, Collin said, "See that slip right next to the ferry?"

"Oh, no," said Andy. "The ferry wake, all day and all night?"

"Let's go, Mr. Cheerful, Mr. Sees the Bright Side of Everything."

Chapter Fourteen

Karen watched Van, her father's assistant, move around the living room taking pictures of her dad's many collections of the things that interested him, including glass jars of shells and sea glass; cabinets of small dolls collected from all over the world. Van wrote notes as he moved silently around the room.

Jared James, her father and Tyler's grandfather, in his quiet and self-contained way, had provided for her and Tyler when they needed help most. The fire not only took the life of her husband and Tyler's arm but sucked the life out of her, destroyed the foundation she lived on, and left her unable to care for her son. Jared, unemotional and methodical, brought her and Tyler into his home, where they leaned on each other and she and Tyler found peace from the nightmare of the past.

But Jared, being Jared, while providing for her and Tyler, focused on the things that he loved rather than people, and that helped turn the museum in Port Tiffany into one of the finest community museums in Washington. Jared never shared openly with herself or Tyler, always carefully and respectfully moving around them, tending to his collections. So she didn't miss her father, as everyone assumed, since his death. She didn't feel now much different than when he was alive. He had shared his home with her and Tyler, and she would be forever grateful for that.

"How's it going?" Karen asked Van.

"I'm probably done up here. Do you think I've missed anything?" He looked at her over his glasses in that solid unemotional way he had.

"I think we have looked at everything I wanted you to look at up here. We've looked at everything on the walls and everything in drawers and cabinets that I had questions about. Let's go downstairs."

Karen turned on all the lights in the basement. The Victorian house stood in the center of the room in a glory of light and it showed all the tender loving care that Jared had placed upon it.

"He talked of this house," said Van. "But I'd never seen it before."

"All the boxes stacked around in this room and the next -- I need to go through them, I think they're full of family stuff," said Karen. "That can all be dealt with later. But, this dollhouse, with seventeen rooms, full of miniatures he collected for it -- this is a massive meticulous job. In fact, I don't want you to move anything, but would appreciate if you would take pictures and do research based on those pictures."

Van's eyes never showed emotion but he did nod that he heard her and he never took his eyes off the dollhouse. His gaze went to the rolling stool that Jared used. He pulled it up and got his camera out. Karen settled into a chair and watched him carefully aim the camera several different directions into each room. He did not touch anything. No wonder he worked so well with her dad. Quiet and efficient, his eyes took in everything.

The dollhouse, built by Jared's grandfather, and cared for and furnished by Jared, silently absorbed Van's attention.

*****

Andy threw his duffel and then his sleeping bag to Collin, jumped over the side of Angel without using the steps, and then walked beside Collin down the dock. Collin and Andy tossed the duffel back and forth as they walked, a good-natured game, but inside, underneath, Collin relished having his boat back to himself. It wasn't that Andy had been a bad sailor, far from it. Andy learned quickly how to handle a sailboat and how to handle himself on someone else's boat. And Andy's generosity of spirit when he, Collin made a major mistake that crashed the boom -- Collin appreciated all of that.

Collin needed to refocus on the goal -- Kingly Island, a summer of sailing and writing his book. This unfortunate and untimely boom problem -- needed his attention so he could be on his way.

When they reached the end of the dock, a woman up on the road waved at them and called out, "Andy! Collin!"

"Who is that?" asked Andy.

"I don't know. I don't know anybody on this island," said Collin.

Collin and Andy approached her. Collin liked the way she looked -- not young, but stylish in her sundress and large hat. She held on to her hat to keep it from blowing off and smiled warmly at them. "I'm Fran, a friend of Mabel's and I told her I would pick up the good pastor for her. I'll bet you're Pastor Andy," she said to Andy and Andy beamed.

Good, thought Collin. Let him be smitten by her and both be off to save Mabel from whatever malady afflicted her. Then she turned to him, and her smile and blue eyes captured him so that he forgot what he needed to say and what he needed to do next.

"And you're the white knight for Andy," she said.

"Huh, sure. Always glad to take credit, whether it's due or not."

Fran and Andy immediately focused on each other, Mabel, and the beauty of the island. He helped get Andy's bags into Fran's car, said goodbye to them and then set off to find what exists in every harbor -- a bulletin board with business cards on it -- business cards of people who repair boats. And he found it, across the parking lot in front of the restrooms and café. A young but heavy set man leaned on the bulletin board and watched Collin approach.

"Hi there," said the man. "I saw you come in. Looks like you need a repair job. Name's Mike."

Collin noticed a yellow rose on Mike's right hand -- a sissy tattoo for a guy like Mike. Collin noticed everything. They talked as they walked back down the down the dock to Angel and then Mike stopped talking. He studied the boat from the dock and then he and Collin climbed onboard. Still silent, Mike looked the boat over thoroughly before he inspected the broken boom. "Just like making sure your boat is worth my time," he said.

Just then the ferry moved noisily out of its slip past Angel, rocking her, and making it impossible for Collin to speak -- saving him from an angry response. Collin, never afraid to pay top dollar for work, did want a good attitude in the other person -- good work and a good attitude before he handed over good money, and this guy's attitude didn't come close. Too bad he hadn't enough time in his life to learn how to work with wood and tools, or he would fix it himself.

Mike focused on the boom and the sail. "Quite a mess," he said. He ran his fingers over the whole boom and then looked out to sea for a long time. "I can fix it in six days."

Collin almost choked. So much for a speedy departure for Kingly Island. "How much?" he asked. Mike quoted a number twenty-five percent higher than Collin thought reasonable.

"Thanks Mike. I'll keep you in mind."

*****

Two phone calls later, Collin again stood on his boat while a man named Peter looked over the problem and gave him a quote. Higher than Mike's.

"I'm the best guy around," the guy said. "Mike give you a quote yet?"

Collin nodded. "Yeah, I've talked to Mike."

"I can do this job fast and you need to know, Mike's done time. I wouldn't want him on my boat."

Later, sitting in the café, Collin thought about his boat and ate a hamburger, the kind of hamburger that he wished he could eat every night -- the kind of hamburger that gives solace and strength in a day. The cook came out to see how Collin liked the hamburger, but he really wanted to know what Collin intended to do about Angel and the broken boom. "Get anybody to fix your boat yet?"

"Does everybody know I've got a broken boom?" asked Collin.

"At least everybody down here in the harbor," said the cook, wiping his hands on his apron. "Be careful of Mike. He's done time."

Collin didn't respond but kept enjoying the taste of his hamburger. The cook thankfully left, and then Andy arrived, sliding into the booth opposite him.

"Some would call that a widow-maker," Andy said with a bright smile.

Collin swallowed the last bite, and then replied, "That's pretty crass, coming from a preacher and seeing as I'm a widower."

Andy's face fell. "Thoughtless of me. Sorry."

Collin pulled out his wallet and handed the waitress his money. "That's okay. Anytime I can see that you aren't so perfect is fine with me."

"I'm more imperfect than you know."

"Hard to believe. Especially since you never married. Marriage reveals to us our imperfections."

"How's it going with the boom fix?" asked Andy. "I just came by to pick up my sunglasses. I think I left them near my bunk on a shelf."

"The boom fix isn't going very fast. I've got to pick between two bids and one is from a guy who evidently spent time behind bars."

"What about the other guy?"

"The other guy wants more money but he'll get it done faster, four days instead of six."

"What are you going to do?" asked Andy.

"I'll get the faster more expensive guy on it. Sometimes that's what money's for."

"Since you'll be here for a few days, do you want to meet Mabel? She's quite interesting."

Collin, quite sure she wasn't, but the time stretched before him for the next few days and he needed to occupy himself in some way, said "All right. Tomorrow."

"I'll get my glasses off Angel and then tomorrow I'll introduce you to Mabel. It'll be an easy walk."

"I don't believe you; I don't trust you. But I have no choice."

Chapter Fifteen

All the concern and attention concerning Mabel seemed overdone to Collin until he met Mabel. Overdone in that a worn-out old lady should never be coddled. Such women, or men, when they got to a certain point in life should be relocated by their families to a closer location where they could be looked after by their families without unduly inconveniencing their families. End of story. For Mabel's son to fuss on and on about Mabel, send Andy, don't send Andy -- instead of taking care of business -- it just wasn't the way Collin did things. Overdone. That's what he thought before, but now that he stood before Mabel, looking into her steely gray eyes, he doubted his assessment.

"I don't get many visitors. My family sent you, didn't they? My family in Port Tiffany?" Mabel rocked steadily on the porch of her cabin while eyeing Collin. Then she turned to Andy. "Why did they have to send two of you?"

"Actually, he brought me up on his sailboat. I thought you might like to meet each other," said Andy.

"That's right, I'm not here to check on you. Andy thought I needed some entertainment while my boat gets a new boom."

"I'm nobody's entertainment. Andy, why don't you show your friend around? Then maybe you can entertain yourselves by helping me out with some chores."

Around the side of the cabin, Andy pointed out the woodshed. "That's how she heats this cabin and cooks. With wood."

"Good grief. No wonder her family wants her out of here. Good thing she doesn't have an outhouse."

"I have something to show you around back," said Andy.

"No. You can't be serious. No. I don't believe it."

Just a few steps further, and there stood an outhouse in back of the cabin.

"No. No. No. No wonder her family wants her out of here. Now I want her out of here. How old is she?"

"She's eighty-eight, and relax. She got indoor plumbing when she figured she reached old age.

"When was that?"

"When she turned eighty-six."

"Fortunate for you, since you're staying with her."

"I'm going to chop some wood. I might not get dinner if I don't. I think she wants some help with her garden."

As Collin returned to the cabin's front porch, he thought how Andy's cheerful demeanor covered up a cold-blooded ability to connect him with needy people, and Collin didn't like it.

*****

"I could use some help with my garden. Do you know how to use a hoe?"

Developing shopping centers demanded people skills, business skills, and an ability to show up frequently on work sites and lend his knowledge and physical presence to the work. Did he know how to use a hoe? And certainly, woven all through his skills and days as a real estate developer, he knew to be slow to get angry. Very valuable part of life, to not let people disrupt his serenity. So, he surprised himself when he leaned close to her and said, "Do I look like someone who hasn't worked with his hands, ever?" asked Collin.

"Yes," she said. "To my way of thinking there are two kinds of people, those who show up here looking to take advantage of me and get control of my property, and those who have some other scheme." She rocked more furiously.

Collin stepped up on her porch and looked out at her view and then replied.

"You can think whatever you want. You do own a beautiful property with a beautiful view. *Now*, I'm going to get the hoe and work on your garden until Andy comes back."

Out in the garden, feeling undignified, he was grateful that she didn't need help with the outhouse or that Andy didn't need help with the wood. He methodically and carefully hoed around each plant and worked hard enough that he worked up a sweat and needed to take off his sweatshirt. He lost track of time, giving every plant attention and enjoying the beauty of the rich earth moving under his hoe and the sound of Andy whacking the wood.

"Well, that's not bad, but if you worked a little faster, you could be done by the time Andy finishes splitting that pile of wood."

How did she do that, sneak up on him and startle him like that?

"Mabel, go back up on the porch and stay there where it's safe."

"How dare you tell me what to do on my own property? Did you know my son is coming in a few days? He doesn't put up with people bossing me around."

He pointed to the porch and refused to work until she backed down and returned to her rocking chair.

As he returned to his work, he noticed a hot steaming cup of coffee she left for him on a nearby stump. He enjoyed the hot strong coffee but did not thank her for the gift. He kept working, and found that when he tried to think about his boat problem or his daughter problem, he couldn't focus on either. His mind went to Kingly Island and the anticipation of serious sailing and writing. The rhythm of Andy chopping wood, the view, and the satisfaction of his own neatly hoed rows lulled him into a better place, until he heard tires on the gravel driveway.

Fran emerged, vibrant red hair falling around her shoulders. "That's very high-powered garden help you have here," said Fran to Mabel.

"I know," said Mabel. "But he's slow and misses spots."

Fran laughed as she bent down to kiss Mabel's cheek.

Andy appeared, eyes on Fran.

Fran, with all eyes on her, addressed Collin. "If you need a break from gardening and chopping wood, I wondered if you and Andy would like to see my gallery. It's on the other side of town."

"I know nothing about art, and I need to finish this job for Mabel -- then I need to check on my boat," he said. Not very gracious, but with all the universe kept putting in front of him, conspiring to keep him from his goal, he would not be enticed by an attractive woman to go look at art. Not going to happen.

Her smile faded, then reappeared. "Maybe some other time, maybe tomorrow?" she said as she put her hand on Mabel's shoulder.

The steel in Collin turned to oatmeal. "Okay. Tomorrow."

Andy nodded. Collin told them he would walk back to town as soon as he finished hoeing. He needed to check on Peter's progress with Angel's boom.

Chapter Sixteen

Collin ran his hand over the broken boom. It lay there broken and untouched. Nothing showed any signs of work. And where was Peter? Was the man dead? Brain dead? He wanted to kick something, but decided that would hurt his foot too much. His eyes scanned the marina, but he saw no sign of Peter. A man with a gray beard down to his chest came slowly along the dock pulling a cart. They watched each other until the man came alongside Collin's boat.

"I hear you got a boom problem," the man said, squinting up at Collin.

"I've got more than a boom problem, I'm missing the man who is supposed to fix the boom problem."

The bearded man said, "My name is Deet. Can I come aboard?"

Collin eyed the man with distaste. Could he not just get this boom fixed and get out of here and on with his project? Did he have to be social with every guy on the island?

He gestured for the man to come on board. Deet, who could barely creep along the dock with his cart, gracefully climbed aboard and started examining the boom.

"Somebody did a bad installation on this boom," said Deet.

"Yes," said Collin. He was not going to admit to this man that he had missed the problem when he bought the boat.

Deet continued to examine the boom, going over the entire structure, including the hardware and the sail. His gnarly fingers touched everything. His fingers looked like the sun had eaten them up and then someone pounded them with a hammer.

"Who'd you hire to fix it?" asked Deet as he faced Collin.

"Peter."

"Sure. I know Peter. He's two docks over, working on that big yacht today."

Collin approached the yacht looking for Peter and saw him on the foredeck. "You want to come down here and talk to me?" asked Collin.

"Weather's great today, isn't it?" said Peter as he stepped onto the dock.

"Don't talk to me about the weather when you owe me an explanation of why you aren't working on Angel," said Collin.

"It's just the way it is," said Peter, standing in front of Collin with his arms across his chest. "This yacht came in after I talked to you, offered me more money to fix a couple of things so they can continue on in a couple of days. You'd a done the same thing."

"No. I wouldn't. I keep my word and do good work. People know they can depend on me."

"Look, I'm sorry, okay? I'll get to your boat in a couple of days. Three at the most."

Collin wanted to punch Peter in the jaw or tell him that he himself had made more money than Peter would ever see in three lifetimes, partly because he worked hard, and kept his word. That's why he could retire young, and Peter would be forever working until his knees gave out -- but Collin didn't say anything. He took a deep breath and then smiled.

"Look. I'm going to get some other help lined up."

"Really? No one else around except Michael."

"Well, when you come back around in a few days, we'll see if you're needed." Collin said it flatly but with finality. He would find someone else on this island to do the work. He didn't want to pay Peter anything. He would figure out how to fix the boom himself rather than pay Peter.

Collin walked back to the café and slid into a booth, aware his girth made sliding difficult. No matter -- he ordered a hamburger and he started reading the ads in the local newspaper. When the burger appeared in front of him Collin saw the muscular male hand partially covered with a yellow rose. Collin looked up to see Michael. "What are you doing here?" asked Collin.

"It's a job," said Michael. "I'm cooking."

"Is it all right if I call you Mike?" asked Collin.

"No." Michael turned and left Collin to his burger.

The man in the next booth turned around. Deet. "Should have hired him," said Deet. "Almost everybody is afraid of him because of his record. But he knows what he's doing on a boat. Better'n anybody."

"I'm surprised they hired him to work here," said Collin.

"Cook's his uncle," said Deet. "They don't get along."

"Oh," said Collin, as if that all made sense.

*****

Julie struggled to read the almost illegible diaries when the hospice people arrived or when May slept. As May continued on her quiet solitary march toward meeting her maker, Julie desperately wanted to know May, but it was hard to weave the pieces together in her fractured days. One day Julie curled up on the sofa and opened the diary to read about May's eighteenth year when her telephone rang -- Faye from New Mexico.

"How are you doing? Staying out of trouble? What's going on with your wrist?" asked Faye.

"It still hurts when I use it the least little bit, but it's better -- I can tell it's better, so I hope I won't need any surgery."

"What about the painting?"

"Of course I missed my chance with Atir, but he said I could try again in the fall." No point in telling Faye about her hopes and joy in painting with her left hand.

"Ricardo's been asking about you. I think he wants to go up there and help you return home."

"That's sweet, but he's quite annoying and I will return on my own. He's just looking for a vacation spot. A cheap vacation spot."

"I hardly think he needs to save money. You're selling him short."

"Come on. Isn't he a parking attendant downtown?"

"That's right. For that big hotel. The one his dad owns."

"Are you serious?" asked Julie.

"Yes. His dad is training him from the ground up to run the hotel."

"Oh."

"Any interesting men up there?"

"Sure. A pastor and a business man -- they're falling all over themselves fighting for me."

"Really?" asked Faye.

"No. They hardly know I'm alive. My days revolve around taking care of May, painting, and, you will not believe this, I've started reading her diaries."

"You're kidding."

"No. I'm serious."

"What kind of diaries?"

"Those five year things, with tiny places to write for one day. Her hand-writing is terrible. It is *slow* going."

"Isn't that an invasion of her privacy?" asked Faye.

"I'm thinking this whole death process is an invasion of privacy as far as I and her caregivers go. We take care of her bodily needs in every way possible. Anyway, I never had much family, and I like knowing something about her before she passes."

"Okay, what are you learning?"

"It's like deciphering a code, that's how bad her handwriting is, and she mainly writes about what she does in a day, mundane stuff, but every once in a while, it becomes interesting -- she complains about somebody making too much noise with his lawn -- things like that."

"I'd be more interested in the entries from her younger years, but let's not talk about that right now. Mind if I may ask a personal question?" said Faye.

"You just lectured me about being too personal with May, and now you want to ask me a personal question?"

Faye sighed and then said, "I'm just wondering how you are dealing with money issues. That's all."

"The court is making sure I have enough money to run the household."

"No other heirs, worried about their share of the loot?"

"Probably just one, her great nephew HH, and he's being a perfect gentleman. He is quite successful in New York as a stockbroker, and he appreciates me taking care of May. No problem there."

"That doesn't seem possible."

"It is possible. Part of my perfect days. Gotta go. Next door neighbor's daughter is coming over for a painting lesson."

"Don't get yourself into trouble. I'm always suspicious when someone talks about perfect days."

"Really. Everything's wonderful. I'm even making progress with my temper. God's healing me with that. And although I'm not interested in a relationship, those two men that I mentioned -- the next door neighbor and the pastor -- they're both very nice and older than me."

"Listen, kiddo," said Faye. "You're missed around here. Don't get overly attached up there."

"No real chance of that. See you later."

Chapter Seventeen

"You could lose a few pounds," said Andy cheerfully.

Collin grunted and walked faster, even though sweat trickled down his cheeks. Soon he would leave Andy, and all these people behind, just like he had left Port Tiffany behind.

"She said she would have refreshments for us. Can you make it?" asked Andy.

"If you weren't a pastor, I might want to physically take your attitude down a notch," said Collin.

Andy laughed and then pointed ahead at the gallery, sitting by itself on a bluff, with wide windows looking down at the harbor.

Fran emerged on the patio and waited for them. Her red curls moved gently with the sea breeze and when they got close enough, Collin could see the exquisite color of her eyes again and warmth of her smile.

"Most people wouldn't dream of walking out here, this far out of town," she said as she greeted them. Collin returned the brief hug, aware of something light and wonderful, like lavender and beach grass, but he quickly sunk into a chair and watched her pour lemonade.

"So how do you get the tourists out here to buy art?" asked Collin as he took in the view of the town and the harbor.

She laughed again -- a tinkling attractive laugh. "I really don't want a lot of tourist traffic. They come in, they take up my time, and they don't buy anything much. I want serious collectors -- often people who have heard about my shop on the Internet. And I specialize in antique miniatures."

"That sounds familiar. Wasn't it Jared James that collected miniature art things? His daughter has to prepare a record of it all for the IRS, I think."

"That's right. We shared that interest. Are you interested in art, Collin?" Fran asked.

"I know nothing about art. I know what I like, but that's it. I actually prefer to hang photographs on walls. Preferably photos of my own real estate projects."

Fran smiled and turned to Andy, who had lost his forever-happy look and just looked at Fran, like he couldn't get enough of looking at her.

"What about you, Andy? Or do you spend all of your time dealing with people and their spiritual and physical needs?"

"I don't know much about art. Maybe you could educate me. Jared never liked to talk about art very much. Although he did show me his prize possession one time."

"Oh, really?" said Fran.

"Yes, his Victorian dollhouse and all those miniatures. He was quite proud of it, and I found out later he didn't show it to just anybody."

"Yes," said Fran. "Indeed."

They ate and continued to talk, and Collin started watching the two of them more closely. They were flirting with each other. They flirted like a couple of high school kids. How old was she anyway? Certainly older than Andy, but her lithe body, her ability to make you feel like you were the only person around when you talked with her -- she was captivating. And Andy seemed smitten by her. Nothing wrong with that. Andy, unmarried, but still a man and Collin didn't blame him for enjoying Fran. As Andy and Fran continued to banter, Collin dropped out of the conversation and realized they didn't care. Not only that, as the time drifted on, they consistently ignored his comments and he saw he added nothing to their time together. Time to go back.

"I've got to go check on my boat," he said as he stood up.

"But you haven't seen my collection of western antique miniature art," said Fran.

"I had to fire the original guy and hire a new one. Time to go see if he is actually fixing the boom." Collin got up, stretched, and moved to leave. "Thanks for the lemonade. You've got a great location up here." Andy and Fran were already moving inside and didn't hear him.

Collin enjoyed the easier downhill walk back into town. He thought about his next hamburger and Michael working on Angel's boom. He would get the hamburger first. His mind went to his daughter Sandy, but only briefly did he wonder about her and what kind of job kept her busy in Port Tiffany. Time to get a hamburger and see Michael.

*****

Retail therapy. A good name for it. HH sorted the mail on his desk, the bill stack far exceeding anything else. Was there no end to it? Why did he give his daughter three credit cards? Why, with all that they owned, did his wife keep shopping? Didn't they have well-decorated homes, plenty of clothes, and enough gadgets in the kitchens?

And where was that irritating little man, Van? Van thought himself such a big shot since Jared James died. Van couldn't soak up enough attention in Port Tiffany, sure, no doubt, that he would get James' job. Such a cocky little guy. Wouldn't make it in New York City for half a day. Slimy even. Maybe the board of directors won't give him James' job. That would be a deal.

Sensing a presence in his den, HH looked up to see his wife hovering at the door.

"Dear," she said in that simpering wispy voice. "Van is here to see you. You know, from the museum."

"Yes, yes. Have him come in."

Van entered the room, but not before he stopped to thank Marileta and tell her how wonderful she looked. HH blocked out their chatter and continued to study the bills on his desk until he could stand no more of their conversation. He stood up, ready to tell them to shut up, when Marileta finally left and Van settled into a chair.

"You're a lucky man," said Van. "Very fine wife."

"Quiet. I don't need you remarking on my wife," said HH as he leaned back in his chair and took out a cigar, thought better about it and put the cigar down.

"I know I'd be proud to have a wife like that," said Van.

"*Shut up* and tell me what you've learned about the painting," said HH.

"I don't like being treated this way," said Van. "I'm a business associate and you need to treat me with respect."

"You're holding back on me. Playing games. You want more money, don't you? You aren't getting any money at all until you tell me what you've done and what you know. That's the deal."

"Money on the table, pal."

HH opened the top desk drawer with a bang, took out a box, and counted from it ten $100 bills. He shoved the bills over to Van, who recounted them and then put them in his wallet. Van sat back down on the edge of the chair as if he might need to take off.

"It's like this," Van said. "I did everything you asked, and then some. I got Karen to trust me. I got her to believe I was the only one who could help her, and she asked me to go through everything in that house, making appraisals. And I did."

"Let me get this straight. You went through the Victorian dollhouse thoroughly?"

"I did. Thoroughly. She watched the whole time. Then I went back four separate times to appraise any and all collections and antiques in the whole house. And I made up reasons to go back and check the Victorian dollhouse two more times."

"And? Did you find it?"

"No. I'm telling you it isn't there."

"*What* do you mean? One little miniature painting couldn't be found?"

"I'm telling you that none of his collectibles are worth much--"

"I don't *care* about whatever else he spent his money on, we're talking about a priceless five-by-seven painting and you couldn't find it?"

"I'm telling you it wasn't in the dollhouse, and wasn't hidden anywhere in their home, either."

"How could you know that? You couldn't possibly know that."

"She got to where she would trust me, and left me alone in the house, and I checked everywhere."

HH's face turned red. He stood up and said, "You mean I just paid you one thousand dollars for *nothing*?"

Van laughed nervously. "I found out something you wouldn't know if it wasn't for me."

"Well what is it? You better have something good or I'll pull enough strings in this town to make sure you never get James' job."

"The parlor and all the rooms in the dollhouse are quite large--"

"*Yes!*"

"And the wall in the parlor, opposite the fireplace, is large and blank. Just two little chairs and a credenza, but the wall is interesting, because it's papered in a miniature print, and the paper is faded around a five-by-seven inch rectangle." Van stood up smiling smugly, but ready to run if HH came after him.

But HH didn't. He sat back and said, "That can only mean the painting was there. I know it was there. It was there at least until that day that I tried to go into the basement with Karen, and Jared, working in the basement, wouldn't let me go see the house. He didn't want me anywhere close to that painting. So, where is it now? Where did he take it?" HH asked himself thoughtfully.

"Like I said, I got Karen to trust me a lot. She told me of the only safe deposit box he had, and what was in it. Some old coins and stamps. I helped her with those."

"Are you sure she would tell you the truth?"

"I'm sure. She likes me."

"Did you get any sense that she knows about the painting?"

"I don't see how Jared could keep it from her."

"That's beside the point. Could you tell by anything she said or did, any nervousness, that she even knows about the painting?"

Van moved to the door as he shook his head no.

"You can't go yet! Where's the blasted painting?"

"Jared James, as far as I can tell, the only place he went, those last few days of his life was to work and back home. Except for one thing."

"And what are you referring to?"

"He went to May's house to have dinner with her and that niece."

"I know all about that, fool. That's when he died. He never got there."

"Oh but he did. That morning he went by the Farmer's Market and bought some stuff and took it to May's house. His contribution to the dinner they were to have that night."

"You're sure about this?"

"Talked to several people who saw him do it. Everyone who mentioned it thought it a bit silly, considering May and everything."

Chapter Eighteen

What might look like a hovel, a shack of little value to the average observer, might actually be the source of great pride to a man, because it housed his precious tools and workshop. Knowing this, Collin stepped optimistically into the worn-out shed behind the café.

Collin ran his hands over the new boom. A beauty, all one piece, one piece of old growth fir, varnished to perfection. Fourteen feet long, four inches-by-eight inches, the boom looked solid and beautiful. Michael knew his craft. This boom would not break. This boom, a prime example of art and function, made Collin smile. Collin couldn't remember seeing any piece of furniture finished to the perfection of this boom. He stood and shook his head in amazement.

"This is great. Good work," Collin said.

Michael smiled and then nervously cleared his throat. "There is one problem going forward," he said.

Collin felt at ease with the world and Michael and nothing Michael said at this point could rattle him. Michael knew boats and the first class work a first class boat warranted. Collin knew people. And Michael, obviously the right man for the job, proved again Collin's good judgment concerning people. Collin still had the magic touch that marks a good businessman.

Fearlessly he asked, "What's the problem?"

"The problem is the sail track," said Michael. "One end got pretty mangled when the boom broke."

"Right, I know that. I assumed you would replace it."

"It'll be expensive," said Michael.

"Money is no problem at this point," said Collin, feeling benevolent and wise.

"That's not the only issue. I've already checked and I can't get one here for two weeks."

Thud.

"Did you say two weeks?"

"That's right."

Collin could feel his dream slipping away again, just like it started to slip away in Port Tiffany. He knew if he hung around Stillwater Harbor for two more weeks, somebody or something would suck him in and destroy his dream forever. People, people, people, wanting time, precious time from him -- all part of the pressures of the universe conspiring to keep him from his dream, keep him from Jan's dream.

"Michael. There has to be another way. I can't wait around here for two weeks."

"I could try to fix it myself. I've got a torch and an anvil -- my buddy's tools of course."

"Michael. I don't need anything else broken. I'm going up to Alaska, where boat repair is limited. I need this to work. Can you fix it so it will hold up to sailing and the weather?"

"Yeah. I can do that. It might not look so good though. I mean it will work and it will look all right, but not as good as a new one."

Collin could see Andy standing at the door of the shed. Andy meant people, their needs, and asking Collin to do something. Collin needed to get going on his trip or forever be pulled by Andy to do something good for somebody else. He shifted his attention back to Michael.

"How long will that take?" asked Collin.

"I don't know. But I can work on it tonight after I finish my shift at the café and see what you think in the morning."

"Let's give that a shot. Do you need any money for anything?"

"No. I've got all the tools right here. I appreciate you giving me this chance, Mr. Matthews. Lots of people around here are afraid to hire me. You weren't."

"Keep doing good work. That's all I ask. I'll come by in the morning. And don't call me Mr. Matthews. It's Collin."

"Sure. I'll be right on this even if I have to work all night."

Collin could still see Andy out of the corner of his eye. What did he want?

"Will you come with me to see Mabel," Andy asked as Collin approached.

"I need to go back and work on my boat. Why does she need me? You're the one good with the ladies."

"That wasn't funny."

"Wasn't meant to be. Thought you and Fran hit it off real well. That's all."

"Too well. I left shortly after you did."

"Nothing wrong with it. You're a single man."

"I don't feel like educating you about being a pastor, a Christian man, or anything else. Will you come with me to see Mabel? Her son arrived today from Port Tiffany."

"Why not? I'll probably never see her again after I leave here."

*****

Steve, quiet, and calm, showed them into his mother's cabin where she sat by the stove, looking innocent and sweet. Wrapped in a shawl, she sipped tea, playing the part to perfection. Did Steve know how abrasive and self-centered she could be? He had to know.

Mabel coughed, and then coughed harder. Collin waited patiently while Steve and Andy both knelt down to help her with pats on the back and soothing talk. Steve gave his mother his handkerchief to cough into. *Christians, especially good at soothing talk, irritating soothing talk.* Collin looked on with a concerned smile. *Let her cough and get out whatever the knot of stuff is.*

When Mabel stopped coughing, she leaned back in her chair. Steve picked up the wadded handkerchief in her lap and showed the contents to Andy and Collin. Blood spattered the handkerchief. Collin froze.

Mabel opened her eyes and she smiled sweetly at Collin. "I'm glad you came," she said.

"That's quite a cough," he said. "Are you sick?" *Keep to business and this will all be over. Always try to sound as if you care, but keep to business.*

"I've coughed up some blood off and on for the last few weeks. That's why Steve is here. He and his wife think I should go to Port Tiffany for some tests."

"Sounds like a good idea," said Collin, nodding.

"I don't want to go, of course. I'm afraid I'll not get to come back."

"She's really not wanting to go, but I can't just leave her here," said Steve, looking concerned, leaning toward his mother.

You don't know her. She's not all that sweet. This is an act. I had no gray hair until I met her, thought Collin. *Except for the blood. Acts don't make blood in handkerchiefs.*

Andy, doing what Andy did best, smiled brightly and said, "That's why we wanted you here, Collin. She likes you, and we think you could help."

Yes, I have a little bit of time and I will help get her out of here and the island will be a better place for it.

"What can I do to help?" asked Collin.

"She says she would go to Port Tiffany if you would take her on your sailboat," said Andy.

"*What?*"

"She's not been on a sailboat for many years, but she would leave the island and go check in with the doctor if you would provide the ride."

No. No. No. "I'm sorry. I don't understand. She doesn't even like me. She said so herself. And the ferry is so easy." Alaska drifted farther away. *This can't be happening.*

"Maybe we should leave you two alone to talk for a few minutes," said Steve. He nodded to Andy and they left the cabin.

Collin knelt down beside Mabel. "I'm really sorry you're sick," he said.

"They don't know for sure. That's why I need the tests."

"Were you a smoker?"

"Yes. Except I quit three years ago."

"You seemed okay the other day."

"If I don't move around very much, I don't cough, and I don't always cough up blood."

"I have plans to go to Alaska, you know. You could go on the ferry and be much more comfortable."

"No. I'm frightened, and I want to go on a sailboat. It would mean so much to me."

"You don't even like me. You said so yourself."

"I've decided I like you now."

Collin sighed. "I have things to do in Alaska."

"There's nothing in Alaska that you can't get right here. Alaska is overrated."

Chapter Nineteen

Hospice recommended putting the hospital bed in the living room, and Julie, wanting to do the right thing, had done that. Visitors came and talked for a while, and May, by being in the living room, could hear the pleasant chatter, and Julie didn't worry about her being isolated.

But, Julie felt the need for a change that morning. The sun just barely showed light in the northeast and she could hear the foghorn down below her as she sipped coffee in the breakfast nook in the kitchen. Yes, she and May needed a change. She put her mug on the kitchen counter and took each of the four kitchen chairs into the living room near May's bed and then contemplated the kitchen table. She tried dragging it with one hand. That didn't work. She took her arm out of the sling, threw the sling on the kitchen counter, and winced only slightly as she used both hands to start pulling the kitchen table out of the kitchen and into the living room. She moved each side a few inches, and then went to the other, back and forth, slowly moving the table out of the kitchen, past May, and into the living room.

Satisfied with that, Julie surveyed the mudroom on the other side of the breakfast nook. With a vision and hard work, Julie cleaned it out, putting the rain boots, mop, and broom on the back porch. With the windows in the mudroom open, May could hear the sounds of the harbor -- the fog horn, the ferry engine starting, the voices of the men working in the boatyard. She could also smell the fresh sea air. Julie turned up the heat so that May would stay warm.

She then took the brake off the bed and slowly pushed May into the kitchen, past the breakfast nook and into the mud room and parked the bed so that if May could see -- she would see the sunrise before her and the patch of fog to her left, and if she could hear, she could hear sounds that she must have loved. The scent of the salt air gently trailed into the room from the open window. After placing another blanket around May, Julie brought back in a kitchen chair, warmed up her coffee, and then sat back down beside May to watch the sunrise.

Julie jerked awake, spilling the coffee into her lap. What a crazy thing to do. She put down her mug and dabbed at the spill on her robe. The sun still only a faint glow in the East, and May slept on. Then she heard it. *What was that?* A scraping sound came from the living room, or from the bedrooms? Her heart raced but Julie sat frozen. What should she do? There, the noise again. Should she call the police or go investigate by herself? Julie silently crept into the kitchen, put down her coffee cup, and picked up a knife.

Slowly, one step at a time, Julie walked to the door to the living room. Looking over the room, she saw nothing out of the ordinary. Across the living room to the hallway and then she stopped again. Bang. The noise, louder this time, came from May's bedroom. Forcing herself to breath, Julie backed up and then turned and ran to the kitchen. With shaking fingers she called 911.

Standing with the knife in her hand where she could see the front door, and May's feet in the mudroom, Julie stood ready to protect her aunt and the house -- her heart pounding relentlessly.

Within two minutes the squad car arrived and Julie watched from the window as one officer quietly started to circle the house, and the other came to the front door. Julie opened it before the officer could knock. May slept on while Officer Barclay searched through the house and then Officer Howard joined them. Julie waited impatiently until they reappeared in the living room.

"Good thing you called us," said Officer Barclay. "We definitely see signs that someone tried to pry open that front bedroom window."

"The noises you heard were either the window or the bucket the person tried to stand on. Looks like the bucket didn't take the weight well and bumped into the house."

"Can you catch the person?" asked Julie, knowing the answer, but hoping for a miracle.

"No clues, can't do anything but put some extra patrols around here. Are you alone? Just you and your aunt?"

Julie nodded.

"One thing you need to be aware of is that when thugs know an older person is ill or dying, they're more willing to break in, not to steal money, but to steal any drugs that might be lying around."

"I do have a couple of prescriptions for my aunt."

"Do you have someone who could stay with you, while you're tending to your aunt?"

"Not really. Hospice people come and go during the day. Just me by myself at night."

Officer Howard spoke up. "It's a big job, what you're doing, and you're probably more tired than you think. You might want to get somebody to spend the nights with you, at least until your aunt passes."

Julie quietly shut the door after them and then returned to the kitchen, holding her head and her developing headache and wondering who, in this town, where she didn't really know anybody, would want to spend the nights with her for the next few days or weeks.

*****

Hanging the bottom sheet on the line in the backyard, Julie enjoyed the sun on her face and the gentle breeze from the strait. Very little pain came from her right wrist, but she favored it. After hanging the pillowcases, she stopped and looked down at the scene below her. Pedestrians scurried toward the ferry. Shoppers wandered in and out of shops. In the distance, a tanker moved slowly toward Seattle. Lost in the wonder of the different shades of blue in the water, Julie didn't hear the footsteps approaching.

"Julie?"

Julie jumped and looked and turned around.

"Sorry, Julie. Sorry I scared you. How are you? I saw the police early this morning. Anything I can help with?" asked Sandy.

"I am jumpy. Someone tried to break into the house. I was actually on this side of the house with May when I heard noises coming from the bedrooms."

Sandy gulped. "That's awful."

"Darn right. Never been so scared. Police got here in a couple minutes, but it seemed like hours."

"What did the police say?"

"They said it was probably someone after drugs, a common problem when druggies hear that an elderly person isn't doing well and likely will have something heavy-duty in the house. They suggested I get someone to spend the nights with me in the house. I'm actually thinking I need to do something else."

Sandy reached into the laundry basket and pulled out the top sheet and handed a corner to Julie. Together they started to untangle it.

"What are you going to do?" asked Sandy.

"I'm thinking I should do what the doctor wanted me to do in the first place," said Julie as they straightened the sheet on the line and started to pin it. "I'm thinking I should put Aunt May in a care facility for her final days, and maybe see if I can stay with Karen and Tyler for a while. They've been kind to me. I'd like to get out of this house."

"Julie, are you worried about the talk -- about you and this house?"

"It's not as if I've heard any, but I can't help but wonder. It might be that HH or I inherit this house and you know, if May isn't here, I don't want to be here. It would look pushy."

"You know, when I first met you, I thought you were terribly inconsiderate, full of rough language and yourself. Now I see you're quite concerned about other people."

"You think that's odd, check this out. I hated being here when I first arrived, but now, I'm getting to like this little harbor town. I'm trying to be pleasant. Hard though."

Julie put the laundry basket down at the back door and motioned for Sandy to take a chair while she herself settled in to one. "I'm not even going to offer you some tea," said Julie. "I just want to sit here and be still for a few minutes. So what's going on with you?"

Sandy drew one leg up and rested her knee on her chin. "I came here to be with my dad. I just needed to be with him, and he's gone.

Gone sailing. Gone to write a book, the book that Mom and he planned that he would write. But he's gone."

"Sandy, you aren't sick are you? Or pregnant?"

"No. Nothing like that. But I did just sort of fall apart at school. It wasn't that big of a deal in retrospect, but at the time, it was the straw that broke the camel's back."

"What happened? Were you hurt?"

"No, but scared more than I can say. After dark, I was taking this painting to one of my professors at the gallery on campus and -- I thought I heard someone chasing me and I panicked and fell. Help came right away. I'll never know if someone really stalked me, but I just fell apart, like crying and scared and upset. I made quite a scene. Bloodied my head, lots of blood. They took me to the infirmary. After that, I just wanted to get away from Seattle, school, and see my dad. I wanted to come here after that and spend time with dad, but he didn't want me here."

"What is the matter with him? He's freaky," said Julie.

Sandy laughed sardonically. "I don't feel good, and I don't know what to do about it. Like I've done everything I needed to after Mom died. I went right back to college and finished that year and this year. But, I didn't get a job like Dad wanted me to. I didn't go to summer school. I just couldn't go any further. I know I've disappointed him terribly." Sandy started to cry, little tears at first, and then steady quiet big tears. She drew up the other knee and encircled her legs with her arms, her head bowed, and tears silently flowed.

Julie let Sandy cry without saying anything. But inside, she used the words most people disapproved of. The smart smooth businessman -- not so smart. She would tell him what she thought of his parenting skills for starters. The sweet Julie faded and the temperamental Julie took charge.

Chapter Twenty

The kid did it. The boom, the varnish -- they looked perfect and the sail track -- how did Michael do it? Not a glitch to be seen. The sail track looked brand new. Michael stood by and let Collin go over everything a second time. Kid deserved a compliment.

Collin stood up, nodded at the boom and said, "Good work. Thought you would get the sail track taken care of, but didn't think you would get it looking brand new. I can't tell there was a problem. You're good."

"Help me get it to the boat?" asked Michael.

"Sure." Collin took the front end, the lighter end, and they started off through the shop. Two other men, working in a corner of the shop, nodded at them as they left. Such was the way of men, to quietly acknowledge big hurdles and dedication to accomplish big things, and no need for a big to do over it -- nods between men acknowledge much. They stepped out into the sunlight and slowly marched past other boats with projects in process, carrying the boom on their shoulders. Most workers stopped as if to briefly honor the passing of the boom and the two men, but in the never-ending work that boats entail, one cannot and must not stop for very long. Such is the work ethic in a boat yard.

Down the ramp they walked and passed Deet, waiting at the bottom where the ramp meets the dock. Deet nodded at them and stepped aside as they passed by. This is good, thought Collin. This is a success and the tide has turned. I am about to have my boat back in working order, I am leaving for Alaska soon, and I am soon going to leave all these incompetent needy people behind.

Michael jumped up on the boat and took the whole boom from Collin. Collin followed suit and together they moved it into position. While Michael held it, Collin guided it into place on the mast and inserted the pin. They then connected the foreword part of the boom, and then fully connected the sail to the boom.

"You want the sail cover on?" asked Michael.

"No. I'll be sailing out of here in a couple of days. It will just be in the way. I'll leave it down below."

Collin couldn't stop grinning. He ran the sail up and down, checked out all the hardware, and moved the boom in each direction. Michael watched quietly. More than satisfied, Collin slapped Michael on the shoulder and went below for his checkbook. Michael deserved good money for his work.

After Michael left, Collin pulled out the cheap cell phone he bought for the trip and called his home to let Sandy know he would soon be on his way.

"Hello?"

Collin didn't recognize the female voice. "Hi, is Sandy there?" he asked.

"Collin, this is Julie, next door neighbor Julie."

"Julie, is my daughter around?"

"No. I'll tell her you called."

"Everything okay in Port Tiffany?"

Brief silence.

"Oh, fine. Little incident with an intruder, but everything is under control."

"What do you mean, intruder?" He didn't like the sound of this, but he didn't want to ask too many questions. Questions could lead to entanglement. No, he really didn't want to know too much.

She kept her explanation short. It sounded unfortunate but benign. Grateful for that, he still noticed her cold voice.

"I'm sure you want to talk to your daughter. She went to run some errands. Shall I have her call you?"

"Yeah. Sure. This cell phone may not work as I leave this area. I'd like to talk to her tonight if possible."

"I'll tell her. And please tell Andy I said Hi."

Andy. *"The better than life" preacher, has captured Julie's interest.* Another brief silence. Julie's face, her fresh pretty face, filled his mind, but he quickly said goodbye and hung up.

As Collin walked back down the dock, he wondered why Julie answered the phone in his house. What was she doing in his house? Why did she bring up Andy?

*****

Where was that phone? Collin heard it ringing, but all the extra canned goods bought for his trip covered every seat and counter top providing a zillion hiding places for the damn phone. The package of tortillas vibrated. Yes, Sandy calling.

"Hi, what's going on? Did you find a job yet?" he asked her as he moved cans and he sat down.

"I'm doing some odd jobs. Nothing spectacular. Main thing is I've moved in with Julie."

"Why? Doesn't she have plenty of help with May?"

"Not at night, Dad. Somebody tried to break into her house a couple of nights ago."

"What does that have to do with you? You could get hurt."

"Dad, the police figure it was someone looking for drugs, you know, associated with an older person. The whole incident scared Julie witless. She even considered putting May in a nursing home, and move in with someone, just to get out of the house."

"This is hard to believe, since she comes across quite tough."

"I know, but I think on top of everything else, this put her over the top. She and I can do this together. We can do this, and it will be okay, and I'll be okay. May won't last that much longer."

"You don't know that. You don't know anything about drug-crazed people." Collin felt his throat tighten up as if being squeezed.

"Dad, you left, remember? You left, just like you left mom and me when it got tough with her illness. So I'm here, and I made this decision and you have no right to an opinion."

"Don't talk to me that way. I did my best, I provided for you and your mother and your disrespect isn't right."

"Dad. I'm sure it isn't. But you left, I didn't, and I'm not about to have this sweet little old lady put in a nursing home for the last days of her life, when all I had to do was be willing to move in for a few nights. I'm willing to do that. I've done that. I'm not afraid. Very much."

"Sandy, you have no sense at all and I'm not sure you ever did--."

Click. She hung up. How dare she?

*****

"You know what? You're a freaking sideshow, Andy!"

Andy didn't flinch.

"You've hardly made any money in your life, you don't have a woman, and you have the audacity to stand there and tell me I need to help Mabel; it would be good for my soul. My soul's just fine. Through my businesses I've helped more people make money and support their families than I can count. That's real help. And you know what? I'm tired. I'm done. I deserve this sailing trip up to Kingly Island and you can't stop me with some whiney guilt-trip argument about an old lady who needs a ride on a sailboat."

"That's not it, Collin -- there's more to life and families than making money."

Collin took a step toward Andy, but Andy held his ground, his feet planted and arms folded over his chest.

"How dare you talk to me that way?" said Collin. "Where was your Jesus Christ when Jan was dying? I said it before, I'll say it again. You're just a freaking sideshow. I leave town in two days for Alaska."

Collin leaped up onto his boat as Andy spoke, "Think about your daughter, think about May, and Mabel. People need you for more than your money."

"Get out of my sight!" yelled Collin. He watched as Andy turned and walked away. Collin sank to his knees, holding on to the rail of the boat, his chest felt tight, and he couldn't breathe. He leaned over the rail and forced himself to breathe, in out, in out.

Slowly, Collin's chest started to relax. Was he having a heart attack? Wouldn't surprise him. But maybe not. He lay down on Angel's deck and stared into the cloudy sky. He watched the clouds move, touch each other, and move silently on, driven by unseen forces. One loud squawking seagull flew overhead. Collin lay on the deck, closed his eyes, and folded his hands over his chest; tears started down his face, slowly and steadily. He didn't try to stop them, but lay there, feeling his heart come into his eyes and his eyes burned with tears.

"You okay up there?"

Collin knew Deet's voice. Collin continued to lay on the deck, but waved an arm at Deet and yelled loudly, "I'm fine."

"That's a funny place to take a nap," said Deet.

"Get lost."

"I can get you a doctor if you want."

"Deet, go away and leave me alone. Or I'll come down there and *beat you up.*"

Quietness settled in again. Collin silently wept until there were no more tears. He then got up on his knees, and looked over the side of the boat, searching for a reflection of himself, wondering what he looked like. He saw no reflection, just ripples of constantly moving water next to the dock. He saw no reflection of himself.

*****

"You're gonna do what?" asked Deet from the next stool. He bent over his coffee as if it might escape, but he looked at Collin through shaggy eyebrows, his blue eyes clouded with cataracts.

"I'm going to go see Mabel," said Collin. He offered no explanation. No indication that he might change his mind about going to Alaska.

"You do a lot of funny things," said Deet.

"You don't know the half of it," replied Collin as he finished his coffee.

"I'm going with you," said Deet solemnly.

"No. You can't walk that far. What do you want to go for?"

"I have a bicycle. I want to go. It'll be a good show."

Collin stood up, paid for his breakfast, and started for the door. Deet threw his money on the counter and hurried after Collin.

Collin glanced at him with disdain as they went outside. "Can't anybody do anything around this island without it being a form of entertainment for someone else?"

"No."

*****

Collin walked faster than Deet rode his bicycle, and, since the old man stopped and chatted with everyone they passed on the road, Collin forged ahead, glad to be alone. The day made no sense, but nothing had for some time. He hoped, when he got to Mabel's cabin, to find her gone already, to Port Tiffany or somewhere or anywhere else. Then he would also be rid of Andy, Stephen, his own daughter, and that foul woman he remembered liking, a long time ago. May. May, who wouldn't die and continued to mess up his life. When he reached Mabel's house, he knocked on the door. No answer. He knocked louder. No answer. Then she appeared around the side of the house.

"What do you want?" she asked.

What indeed? Was this any way to greet him?

"I came for a visit."

"I have no time for a visit. I'm hanging out laundry. I'm not a rich retired big shot businessman."

And why was he here? He couldn't remember. He followed her back around the side of the house to the clothesline and the half full laundry basket. She handed him a wet towel and pointed toward the clothespins hanging in a bag on the line. They kept working until the basket was empty.

"Have you ever hung laundry to dry before?" Mabel asked, as she sat down on a stump in the yard.

"Sure. If you count rinsing out socks and hanging them out to dry in hotel rooms."

"Am I supposed to be impressed with you once again pointing out that you've traveled around the world, maybe more than once, and made lots of money?"

"Look. I'm actually quite a humble guy."

"That's a laugh. How do you define humble?"

"Look, it's been my life. Whether you approve or not, it's been my life, and I think I've done a lot of good with it. Quite a number of people have been able to pay their mortgages because of me. But I don't expect you to appreciate that." He sat down on the stump next to her.

"Well maybe I do appreciate that. But maybe I want you to know I've worked hard. My husband worked hard and I don't think you know anything about our lives."

"You are absolutely right. I don't. I'm stupid. And I don't care a thing about you. And I'm sitting here, wondering why I'm here helping you hang laundry, and why I'm about to offer you a sailboat ride back to Port Tiffany."

Her fat little cheeks dropped with that statement. Silence. Good. No, she wanted to say something.

"I don't believe you."

"Don't care if you believe me or not. I'll need to talk to Andy and your son."

"Why would you want to do this? Reality is, we were wrong to ask you, and I need to face my own reality. Once I leave here, I won't be back. So, I ask you again, why would you volunteer to take an old lady on a sailboat ride? Likely her last."

"And I'll say to you, for the last time, it's none of your business."

Chapter Twenty-One

As Steve drove toward his mother's cabin, he wondered, not for the first time, what planet his mother dropped from. Not that his growing up had been bad. His dad, a banker, a stable serious man, had insisted on raising his family in Spokane, and his mother kept up with all four kids, charity work, and loved his dad. After forty-three years of marriage, dad died of a heart attack, but the kids were all making their way, and Mabel, for the first time in her life, unhinged.

Mabel put the house up for sale and called the kids to come get anything and everything they wanted. On her sixty-fifth birthday, with all property and finances simplified, she kissed each of her children, told each grandchild to mind their parents, and then informed them all she intended to sail around the world, on a variety of boats, commercial and private, and she would be back in a year or two.

After listening briefly to their loud protests, she told them all to be quiet, and when they saw her determination, they quickly pushed for sophisticated communications equipment and demanded constant communications and assurances of her whereabouts and well-being. Once again, Mabel would have none of it. She told them her lawyer would know where she was at any time, and would be able to get money to her if she needed it -- otherwise, for the rest of them, they would hear from her via postcards. Possibly.

Brief silence. More squawking.

Still squawking, Mabel showed them the door.

Two years later, Mabel, having successfully sailed on actual sailboats and freighters around the world, surfaced on Bailey Island, between Canada and Washington State. She bought a cabin in Stillwater Harbor, a rustic cabin without indoor plumbing, and she gardened, visited sick people on the island with homemade soup, volunteered at the library, and -- she had no intention of leaving.

Over the years, Mabel welcomed family to the island, and offered hospitality including a place to pitch a tent in her yard, but she never left the island -- not for family events or any other reason. And so the years rolled on, and Steve and his siblings quit trying to convince their mother of anything, and they quit trying to convince their own children and grandchildren of anything about their mother.

For all those years, Mabel had gotten her way. So was it too much to ask of her to be reasonable and adult and think of him, her now aging son, and make some grownup decisions. Evidently not. She continued to think only of herself. She was behaving like a brat.

What would he do without Andy? Andy and Collin, volunteering to spend all day with her on a sailboat, so that she could have this, what would likely be her last adventure on the water. Of course he wanted the best for her, but enough of this time-consuming effort to help her have an adventure when the rest of the family had lives to lead and bills to pay. Andy's patience and whatever it was that made Collin change his mind about Alaska -- all that was beyond Steve.

Steve opened the door to his mother's cabin without knocking. Mabel, Collin, and Andy sat there, looking stoic. "*All right*! Are we ready? A day at sea? Everybody *happy*?" asked Steve.

"Let's do it!" said Andy as he jumped up and picked up the small bag Mabel would take on the sailboat.

Mabel stood up. "Can I talk to you a minute alone?" she asked, motioning toward the bedroom.

Once inside, Steve closed the door and turned to his mother. Her expression told him something bothered her. "What's wrong?"

"I don't think they are really happy about doing this. You know, the Bible says the Lord loves a cheerful giver."

"*No*, Mother. Don't even go there. You wanted this and they volunteered and don't you even think to criticize them for their attitude or even think about changing your mind. You will get on that boat with them and be gracious. I have your other things packed and in my car. I will get on the ferry, go to Port Tiffany, and be there to pick you up when you get there later this afternoon. And you will be gracious and you will be pleasant to them and do what they say."

Wide-eyed, she blinked.

"Do you *hear* me?"

She nodded.

"Okay then. Let's get you on the sailboat. I think her name is Angel."

*****

Steve stood on the dock and waved at his mother, who sat in the cockpit, wrapped in a blanket, appearing innocent and small. What a lie, thought Steve. *Troublemaker*. The diesel engine hummed reassuringly as Collin focused on keeping the boat next to the dock. Andy untied the last line to the dock, threw it on board, and then jumped on board. Collin then steered the bow out away from the dock and Angel moved through the boats toward open water.

Out of all those people, the strangest, by far, was Andy. How Andy could be so patient with Mabel, not even his own mother, was beyond Steve. Collin was hard to figure out; his own mother was a continuing problem, but Andy -- definitely off the charts. Steve's wife often asked him to go to church with her, but he usually found something else he needed to do. It seemed to him that most people went to church on Sunday, but their lives were just like everyone else's. Andy certainly went the extra mile for people, walking like he talked. Steve would give him credit for that. Andy was a lot more peaceful and joyful than most people.

The boat glided out of the harbor. Steve returned to his car. He had just enough time to catch the ferry.

Chapter Twenty-Two

Collin carefully guided Angel between the boats and out of the harbor. He paid no attention to Mabel, who sat quietly beside him, or to Steve, who stood on the deck near the bow, watching for any problems. The sound of the diesel gratified Collin -- a powerful sound, an enjoyable sound. He did not think of how odd it was that he was headed south instead of north and he did not have any remorse. Once he decided on something, he put his mind to it and that was it. On this day, once he got through the islands, he would be crossing the Strait with passengers. He took that responsibility seriously and focused.

Andy came back to talk to Collin. "When will you put her under sail?" he asked.

"Thought I would wait until just before we enter the strait." He turned to Mabel. "That sound all right to you?" he asked.

She smiled.

"Are you warm enough?" asked Andy.

She nodded.

Andy returned to the bow and sat down with his legs hanging over the side of the boat. Mabel, wrapped in her blanket and lost in her own thoughts, sat silently, and Collin steered the sailboat past a Washington State ferry going the other direction. The sun played between the clouds and the green thick forests on each island showed little signs of man. Andy raised an arm, pointing to his right, and Collin and Mabel followed his direction, seeing a whale blow. Collin moved the boat closer to the whale and they watched it silently move into a small inlet. Mabel smiled at him, a thank you for the experience. Maybe she wasn't so hard after all. He turned again, passing near the dark green thick forests on the shore, ever watching his depth sounder to avoid rocks and shallow water. Andy pointed again, this time to a black bear on the beach. Collin watched in wonder until the bear disappeared into the forest.

*****

Andy left the bow and again climbed back to Mabel and Collin. He hung on to the boom as he said, "This is great! Should I fix us some lunch before we put the sails up?"

"How about it, Mabel? We can provide you with a chicken sandwich and a cup of coffee -- then we'll put the sails up for a real sailing experience."

"That's what I came for!" she said.

"I'll get us something to eat right now," said Andy. He disappeared inside the boat. He could have cooked a complete meal, but pulled out the hot coffee and sandwiches brought on board from Stillwater Harbor Café.

Andy was almost ready to take the food on deck when he saw Collin peering down at him. "We have a problem," said Collin. "A big problem."

"Like probably our little ancient passenger needs to go to the bathroom?" asked Andy.

"How did you know? I've never dealt with something like this before," said Collin, looking worried.

"No big deal. Get the boat slowed down and on auto pilot, then you will literally hand her to me, and then you will come down here, we'll help her and it will all be easy."

Collin's expression said he wasn't so sure, but he secured the boat, helped Mabel walk to the ladder, and then he wrapped Mabel even more securely in the blanket and then picked her up and handed her down to Andy. Collin quickly looked around and then also went below. The movement of the boat was gentle, but they both held onto her until they reached the head.

"There's plenty to hang on to in there," said Collin.

"I can manage! I'm not a baby," said Mabel as she shut the door.

"I'm going back up," said Collin.

When the door opened and Mabel reappeared, she found Andy waiting for her.

"I'm going to walk by myself back to the ladder," she said. And she did, finding something to hold on to every step of the way. She stopped and looked at the lunch.

"I see you bought lunch. I could have made us something in this galley," she said. "I know how to do things on a boat. I've sailed more than you two guys will ever sail."

"So true," said Andy. "But it's my job for today and you're going back up with Collin. I need you sitting safely on deck by Collin. I intend to deliver you all in one piece to your son."

"I don't think so," said Mabel. "I'm going to stay right here and help you do whatever needs to be done. This is a lovely boat and a beautiful galley."

"For the love of God, get up the ladder, Mabel!" said Andy.

"Whoa, so the pastor has his flash point," said Collin, peering down at them.

"I never did think he was as nice as he pretends to be," said Mabel.

Andy put his face within six inches of hers. "Get up that ladder, sit down, and wrap yourself in that blanket, or I will throw your sandwich overboard."

*****

Collin stood at the helm, the wind filled the sails perfectly, the boat sliced through the water, directly aimed at Port Tiffany. Couldn't ask for better wind. Mabel, wrapped up in the blanket and totally still, seemed lost in her own world. What was she thinking? Her face lifted slightly into the wind; she smiled a private smile. With memories of what? No doubt memories of far off places and people from her grand sailing trip. Maybe she thought of her husband and raising kids. She looked innocent and small, her gray curls dancing in the wind. Collin quit thinking about her and concentrated on sailing the boat.

A large tanker passed in front of them, and then a submarine. Small fishing boats dotted the water. Andy climbed up the ladder to stand beside Collin.

"Great sailing weather," said Andy. "You want me to put more sail out?"

Collin nodded. With more sail, Angel picked up speed, and Collin felt the joy only sailing gave him. The boat leaned more, but instead of being frightened, Mabel smiled -- a dreamy smile that probably reflected pleasant memories.

Andy sat down beside Mabel. "Is this the experience you wanted?" he asked.

She smiled at him and pulled the blanket closer. "I'm loving this. Thank you so much."

"Are you remembering your fantastic trip around the world?" asked Andy.

"Yes, but also the sailing I did with my husband."

"Really? I thought he didn't sail."

"He used to take me out on a little lake near Spokane, in a tiny little sailboat, barely room for two people."

"Wow, I didn't know that -- so that's how you came to love sailing."

"Yes, but the problem was he never loved it. He started on a suggestion from one of his employees. He thought it would be a great way for us to connect with nature, and a great way to add to our future kids' lives. But, he didn't really like it, and when the kids came along, he was too busy, and it all went into my memory basket."

"Kids never picked it up?"

Mabel laughed. "No. And I thought it important to nurture whatever they were about, and none of them showed much interest in sailing. But it was a gift my husband gave me, for a short while, before life got so very busy. He gave me a taste of it."

Collin had listened carefully to their conversation, and when she went quiet, he didn't add anything. The three of them, each lost in his or her own thoughts, feeling the quiet power of Angel, the water, the sun and the breeze on their faces, moved closer to Port Tiffany. But that moment didn't last long.

"Is there anything else we can do?" asked Andy.

"Well..."

"Just name it."

"The part of my trip going through the Panama Canal, there was this extraordinary thing."

"What was it?"

"Hot chocolate. There were just ten passengers, and I remember going through the canal, the loveliness of the scenery, and that hot chocolate."

Andy looked at Collin. "Do you have any hot chocolate on board?"

"Uh, maybe," said Collin. "Look in one of the canisters. Might be some envelopes. I think I saw some, but they likely have been there a long time."

Just as Andy started down the ladder, Mabel said, "Hot chocolate flavored with peppermint."

Andy sighed and looked helplessly at Collin. "Flavored with peppermint?"

Collin kept his hands on the wheel and shook his head. "I don't think so. But, there might be some peppermint candies leftover from restaurants. Tucked away somewhere. That's all I can think of."

Andy stepped back over to Collin and whispered, "Been really nice if she would have let us know about peppermint flavored cocoa yesterday." Collin nodded and Andy climbed down the ladder to the ship's galley.

To Collin's amazement, Mabel remained quiet while she waited, and soon Andy reemerged with the cocoa.

"Looks like you found what you needed," said Collin as he took a mug.

"Yep, even the peppermint. Found it stashed in the back of a junk drawer." Andy then turned to Mabel and asked, "Is there anything else we can do to help you have a grand experience today?"

The man had an annoying inability to simply let quietness reign. As far as Collin was concerned, Andy had no right to complain about Mabel's requests when he seemed to prod the woman into making them.

Mabel smiled at him and took another sip of her cocoa. "It's just like the old days. Except for one thing."

"What's that?" asked Andy.

"We would sing," she said shyly.

"Really? You're used to sailing and singing? Together?"

She nodded.

"Like what?"

She cleared her throat and started softly, "I'll sing you a song, a good song of the sea, Way! Heh! Blow the man down!" She stopped and looked up at Andy with large hopeful eyes.

Collin's amusement rivaled his annoyance. Mabel had truly

mastered every manipulative tactic known to mankind.

"I know that. Old sea chantey." And so they continued on together. "And trust that you'll join in the chorus with me; give me some time to blow the man down."

Collin remained silent, but watched them in amazement. After a while he joined in with them and the three sang verse after verse, and after a while, Collin's cheeks glistened with dampness, but there was no mist, no spray from the boat. The heartaches from the past, his inability to be with Jan in her final months, to not just say he loved her, but to show her -- all filled him with grief.

"There was an old skipper, I don't know his name, "Way! Hey! -- Blow the man down! Although he once played a remarkable game, give me some time to blow the man down."

Angel moved closer to Port Tiffany, and they sang, the verses, the chorus, over and over again, "Way! Hey! Blow the man down! He whistled all day, but in vain for a breeze, give me some time to blow the man down."

Chapter Twenty-Three

The wind, stronger than the outgoing current, kept Angel on course as she entered the bay. Port Tiffany lie directly ahead and all looked easy. Everything seemed peaceful and spiritually right. But then Mabel spoke.

"Docking a boat can be tricky. I hope you boys know what you're doing."

Ignoring Mabel, Collin said to Andy, "Andy, I'm going to start the diesel before you take the sails down." Andy nodded.

Collin turned the key and pushed the button down, and smiled at the familiar comforting sound of the diesel starting. But then it sputtered, coughed, struggled, and then died.

"What's the matter?" Andy yelled back to Collin.

"I don't know." He tried to start the engine again. Nothing. Again, nothing. A fourth time, nothing. What a terrible time for a failure.

No luck. "Must be a plugged fuel line or contaminated fuel!" he said to Andy.

Andy, who had been standing by the mast and did not look so cheerful, climbed back to the stern and stood beside Collin.

"Have you ever docked a sailboat under sail?" asked Andy, quietly, so that Mabel couldn't hear.

"No. But we have no choice," said Collin.

"We could anchor out here in the bay and radio for help," said Andy.

"Are you guys talking about going in under sail?" asked Mabel. "I think you should--"

Collin interrupted her. "Not now, Mabel."

Collin quietly looked at the wind, the sails, the current, and the trajectory toward the fast-approaching dock at Port Tiffany. Somebody waved from the fuel dock. At him? Was it Steve?

"We've got to go in under sail!" he said. This would test Andy and himself.

Under Collin's direction, Andy moved to the bow and took down the forward sail. He adjusted the angle of the main sail as the wind filled it, and silently they continued on to the dock. Somebody again waved at them from the fuel dock. Yes, it was Steve waiting for them.

Collin gauged the wind and the current as they steadily approached the dock. Then Collin remembered. "Andy, get the fenders down!" Andy nodded and scurried to drop the three fenders over the side of the boat. The momentum of the boat continued, Collin not wanting to ram the dock, but knowing if he didn't keep going, he had no chance of docking.

He could see Steve better now, and he could see Steve's tenseness. Steve knew the consequences if they didn't get Angel docked the first try.

A small fishing boat, coming out of the marina in the middle of the waterway, quickly moved to the side to avoid Angel.

Forward, forward, forward into the marina, and then when a collision with the dock looked certain, Collin called out "Drop the sail!" Andy dropped it and it fell in a heap and the boat pushed forward in a mighty last surge. Andy threw the bowline to Steve who grabbed it, quickly wound it around a cleat while Andy made a mighty leap to the dock, and ran back to the stern, where he caught the line that Collin threw to him.

Andy pulled the stern closer, using all of his strength, and then tied the line off on the cleat.

Collin stood overlooking the scenario, waiting for his heart to slow down. Then he remembered Mabel. She sat totally silent, wrapped in her blanket. He bent down and looked into her eyes. "You okay?" he asked. She nodded.

He heard someone clapping. He looked around the dock and saw an old man, a wrinkled man who looked like he had seen many sailing days, and the man slowly clapped. Collin nodded at him.

*****

Mabel stood on the dock, surrounded by the three men. Collin thought she looked strangely tiny and for her to not be talking seemed stranger still.

"Mother, did you have the adventure you wanted?" asked Steve. He held his mother's bag in one hand, as he tried to get her to talk. It was time to go to her new home, and face the doctors and life on life's terms.

She continued to stand silently among the three men. If they expected a big thank you from her, they weren't getting it. Collin didn't know whether to hug her or tell her to get going with her son.

"I'll walk to the car with you and Steve," said Andy. But Mabel didn't move.

"I need to talk to Collin alone," said Mabel. After Steve and Andy had walked away, she turned to Collin. "I know you gave up a lot to bring me here, this way. I do appreciate it. I know you gave up a lot."

"Well, I did have another reason."

"You think you're pretty tough, but I know tears when I see them," she said.

"You're not so tough either, when you're not being so mouthy."

"Can you just be pleasant to an old lady?"

"I don't know -- I doubt it, but I'll probably be around to see how you're doing."

*****

Tyler stared at May. Sandy stood helplessly and watched him watch May, who was closer to the end, but still breathing. "Do you want some coffee?" Sandy asked. Tyler nodded. She motioned toward the kitchen.

Sandy poured two cups and then sat down beside Tyler, and after another long silence, she finally asked the question. "What happened to your arm?"

"You mean why do I have only a part of my left arm?"

"Yes, Mr. Sensitive."

"I like to be clear about things. People want to ask me about something, they need to be clear."

"So. I'm asking."

"It was a fire."

"And?"

"What's the matter with you? I said it was a fire, can we leave it at that?"

"You are so irritating!"

"*Heh*! You two, come *here*!" Julie stood in the doorway and motioned for them to come closer.

She directed them into a corner as far away from May as she could and said, "What is the matter with you? May is dying, and she deserves some peace and quiet, and you two are bickering. Unbelievable."

"Yeah, well maybe it's my fault," said Tyler.

"As I recall, the two of you made a pact to do odd jobs for people this summer, and I suggest you get with it," said Julie firmly.

"The problem," said Sandy, "is we don't have a job for the next two days."

"Well, cry me a blue moon. Go out and find someone to help that can't pay and leave poor May and me alone. Work out your problems. Yell at each other if you want. But in this house, keep your voices down. I've got laundry to do. Go out on the porch and do your talking there."

Sandy and Tyler hardly got through the door before they squared off. Sandy eyed Tyler with the distaste she felt. "Why don't you like me? I thought we were becoming friends."

"I don't like you because you have everything I would like to have. A start on an education. No real money worries. This wanting to work at odd jobs this summer is a joke for you and I know it."

"You have no idea about my problems, money or otherwise. I've got problems."

"Yeah, well you're spoiled."

"Oh, fine. Let's play ain't it awful. Your life and its hardship are worse than anybody else's, so no one else counts. That really sucks, you self-centered twerp."

He had nothing to say, but only for a moment. "Self-centered? You and your dad come sweeping into this town with plenty of money and a beautiful boat. You make me sick."

"I get it about your arm. That's big. But you are still a self-centered twerp."

Julie appeared again. "What is the matter with you two? Get away from the door and the window, I can hear you in here and I'm fed up with both of you."

Sandy and Tyler stomped down the steps and then faced each other again. "I lost my arm and my dad in a fire. And we lost our farm at the same time. That trumps whatever hardship you've had to face," said Tyler.

"*Shut up*! You freak. Don't talk to me that way. Don't talk to me as if my life doesn't count!" Sandy ran back up the steps, picked up a pillow from the porch swing, and then threw it at Tyler, who stoically took the blow with a smirk.

"I'll ask a third time. *What* is the matter with you two?" asked Julie, standing at the door again. "Sandy, your dad is going to be arriving with the pastor and their passenger this afternoon. Maybe you should figure out what you're going to tell him about how you spent this day. I assume part of the reason he's coming home is because of you."

Julie fixed her gaze on Tyler. "And you, would you please remember that May is dying and I need this house to be peaceful. And it was peaceful until you arrived this morning. Both of you get out of here and go solve your problems somewhere else."

Julie shut the door firmly. Sandy sank down onto the lawn and listlessly picked at the grass. "She's right. My dad is coming back today, and the last thing I want is for him to be mad at me. I told him you and I would be busy all summer. That would be my job, and even though we don't have a job lined up for today, I've got to be busy. Doing something."

Tyler sat down beside her. "Well, at least you've got a dad to worry about," said Tyler.

Sandy whirled and faced Tyler. "Will you please, for one moment, drop that, and can we figure out what worthwhile thing we're supposed to be doing today? You could also remember that you have a mom."

Tyler's gaze dropped and he didn't respond for several seconds. When he did, his voice had lost its combative tone. "My mother did say something about the church needing more room for the kids Sunday school classes."

Something about Sunday school teachers loving and teaching kids, and wanting a pleasant place for those kids pulled at Sandy's heart. "What do you mean?" she asked.

"There are a couple of rooms used for storage -- if they were cleaned out, that would be good space."

"We can't possibly do that." She hit him on his shoulder, got up and started walking toward the street. He followed her.

"Why'd you do that? What do you mean?"

"You're missing part of your arm, you have no dad. My mom died, and my dad hates me. We couldn't possibly be capable of cleaning out a couple of rooms in a church to help some kids."

"You're really dark, you know. Or sarcastic," said Tyler. They walked down the street toward the church.

Chapter Twenty-Four

Collin threw his bag down on the floor and looked around his silent house. What to do next? These people things always had him perplexed and Andy, frequently getting him into a new people dilemma, gave him little guidance on how to handle such situations. Not, of course, that he, Collin actually asked for advice or made it clear in so many words that he was distressed in a situation. But that was beside the point. Andy did suggest that Collin just go home and take one step at a time. Okay, here he stood.

Sandy now lived at May's house -- did that make sense? A young woman and a middle-aged woman, living in the same house with a dying elderly woman, where there had been at least one attempt to break into the house. What was he, the big male, supposed to do with that? The next step was what? Stay here, by himself, in his own house? Probably he needed to move into May's house, sleep on the couch in the living room, and then he could protect the women from anything and everything. But first, he needed food.

Collin opened the refrigerator with anticipation but found nothing. From a cupboard he retrieved a protein bar, and while eating it, he peered out the window at May's house. Where was Julie? He wanted to see her more than his daughter. He used to enjoy looking out the window, waiting for May to appear on the back porch, and now he peered out the window, wanting to see Julie, but he saw no one. Be a man and go knock on the door. But which door? The front or the back? For a man used to traveling the world and doing business with the rich and powerful, he was totally flummoxed by Julie and which door to knock on. He continued to eat his bar and contemplate Julie and the doors when he saw the back door move.

Julie appeared on the back deck with a watering can. As she moved about watering the potted plants, he couldn't see her very clearly through the arbor and the climbing roses, but he suddenly appreciated her beauty, her shiny hair, the yellow t-shirt, and then, just like Andy had said, he knew the next thing to do. He took a shower, shaved and changed his clothes. Looking at himself in the mirror, Collin sucked in his gut and then knew the next thing to do. He marched across the lawn to the neighbor's front door and knocked.

"Wow, so you made it home?" said Julie with an easy smile. He couldn't think of what to say. She motioned for him to come in and Collin noticed that she smelled of lavender as he walked by her. He did not stop until he reached May's bedside. He gently touched her frail hand.

"May, I've been out on the water, sailing. You would have liked it, a brisk wind and clear skies. I even had an older lady on board. Not as pleasant as you, but she and Pastor Andy and I, we had a good time." May slept peacefully on.

As they settled in to the kitchen table, Julie poured coffee for them

"How much longer do you think she has?" asked Collin.

"Maybe a couple of weeks. But of course I think we were saying that days ago. She's tough. Hospice nurse says she's very tough."

"She's got a mind of her own. How's your arm?"

"It's better. Every time I try to use it, it hurts less. I take the splint off once in a while. Still hoping to avoid surgery."

"Still painting?"

"Of course, and actually loving it more."

"You seem awfully calm, even joyful for someone obviously in a financial bind."

"I'm trying some things that Andy suggested, one being to trust God more, and although I'm not totally convinced God is there and interested in my life, my days are going better. I am collecting information."

"By saying God, I presume you mean the Christian God, the trinity, Jesus, and the Holy Spirit?"

"That's right. I'm looking at the whole package."

So. She's been spending more time with Andy than I thought, Collin said to himself. *Crafty, that preacher.*

"How was your shortened Alaska trip?" asked Julie.

"It was not ideal, but I'm here, and wondering about my daughter, and how the two of you are making it. Any more attempted break-ins?"

"No. But I do appreciate your daughter being here."

"It seems like a man is needed. Like I should move in."

Julie choked on her coffee and then laughed. "You're too funny for words. Not that I don't appreciate you're wanting to do the manly thing, but between leaving the outside lights on all night, Julie and I taking turns sleeping out here on the couch close to May, and the sheriff driving by several times at night, I think we have it covered."

"Don't you want to put in an alarm system?"

"Not really. Not now. Keeping track of codes, etc., I don't need it."

"I think you do. But you should at least have my phone number on speed dial."

"I agree with that."

"You do?"

"Don't be so surprised. I'm a reasonable woman."

"What about a dog?"

Julie shook her head. "Not a bad idea, but I don't need to be taking care of a dog, especially since I'll be leaving in a few weeks."

It was a standoff. He had given up so much to return to Port Tiffany and hadn't got much appreciation for the effort, been laughed at, and was not being treated as heroic in any way. He didn't know what to make of it or what to do next. Even though she had laughed at him, it felt good to be in her presence and he desperately needed to find a way to remain there.

She broke the silence. "Your daughter went off with Tyler. They do that most days, taking on odd jobs." Collin nodded. He would deal with his daughter later. He waited. Andy had talked about listening for the still small voice of God. Where was God? The silence, long and big, frightened him.

"I actually found May's diaries. What a writer. She's been writing in those little tiny five-year diaries since she was 16. Then I felt guilty. But it sort of nags at me. I'd like to read more, while I'm waiting."

Bingo. "I don't see a thing to feel guilty about. What greater gift to her, to have you care enough to read and try to understand her life." Collin smiled; he knew he made points with that statement.

"What a lovely thing to say."

Jan had been the only woman who ever actually appreciated him and the way he looked at life and its issues and Jan never tried to change him. But Julie pleasantly had gotten under his skin. She had been quite abrasive at first, but not now. He wasn't sure what she thought of him, but he knew he felt more alive when he was around her, and to make that happen, now that he had returned, was his goal. Collin sat up a little taller. "I could come over during the day and help you read through the diaries. I liked her."

"Wow. Two snoopy people would be better than one?"

"Right."

*****

Collin, with the best intentions to stay awake until his daughter showed up, lay horizontal on the couch with a book on his chest, oblivious to the world. Jan and Sandy had always teased him about how he would warn them to be quiet because he was reading, but they would find him shortly thereafter asleep with a book on his chest, and that was how Sandy found him when she came in the door.

He heard a voice. "Dad." He did not respond. He felt someone touch his shoulder which instantly sent him up, the book tumbling to the floor. Collin looked at his daughter with unseeing eyes.

"Sorry," she said.

He blinked. She leaned down and gave him a kiss on his cheek. He blinked again. She sat down awkwardly beside him.

"Did you have a good trip?" she asked.

"Sure. Great sailing all the way across the Strait. I went to see Julie. I volunteered to stay in the living room and protect both of you."

"You mean all three of us."

"Sure. Right."

"Well, I'm glad your home. I'm glad you're just a few feet away, but it would be unnecessary for you to be right there. That would be a lot of traffic in one bathroom."

He rubbed his eyes. "What did you do today? You and Tyler making any money?"

"Isn't that what's always on your mind?" she snapped.

"Look, I'm interested in your welfare and I'm here. And I'm half asleep. Could we stop with the critique of my every word?"

"All right. I agree. Tyler and I spent the day cleaning out a room at the church -- they need more Sunday school space."

"Pastor Andy cuts a wide swath with my family, keeping my daughter busy and keeping me busy. And it's amazing who he knows."

"Like what do you mean?"

"He's friends with an art dealer in Stillwater Harbor. She's an expert in miniature paintings, especially those that came out of this area in the 1800s. Got quite an education from her, especially about one artist named Bierstadt."

"Was she pretty?" asked Sandy.

Collin nodded. "Extremely so. A little older than me, quite a fun person to talk to, and quite attractive."

"That's the first time I've heard you talk about a woman since Mom died," said Sandy "Did you want to ask her out on a date?"

He stood up and stretched. "I think the good pastor Andy might. They seemed to enjoy each other's company. A lot." He wasn't about to tell her that it was Julie who drifted more and more into his mind. He didn't know her; he couldn't even say he liked her, but he liked being in her presence.

"I came to say hi and get some clothes," she said as she stood up. "I'm glad you came home."

He thought about hugging her, thought better about it, and nodded. "Just remember to call me for any little thing. Tomorrow, Julie and I are going to read some of May's diaries."

"Really? I can't imagine you doing that, Dad."

"The woman had a private life; she's about to leave this planet, and I think it is a good way to acknowledge her life. To honor her. And there is another reason."

"Tell me," said Sandy.

"She mentioned to me that she hadn't been treated fairly in this town. She never made it clear what she meant, but maybe I'll find out by reading the diaries."

Sandy started for the door, but without turning around, she said, "I can tell you like her."

So, she knew. He hadn't disguised it from her. "Do you mind me spending time with Julie? Someone other than your mother?" he asked.

"I meant May," Sandy said and left the room.

*****

The next morning, while Julie and the hospice nurse tended to May, Collin sat on the couch and stacked May's diaries in front of him. The first five were old and fragile, the pages meant for one year, one-day entries. The pages, yellow and hard to read, still looked interesting to Collin. The others, five-year-diaries, he grouped by decades and as he contemplated the diaries and what kinds of mysteries they might hold, he knew what he really wanted to do was lie down on the couch and read, but if he did that, he would likely go to sleep, and that would look like he didn't take the job seriously. He picked up the oldest diary and started reading, reading about May's early years, her father logged for a living, and then her father's death in a logging accident when May was sixteen. After that, her mother supported May and her brother by working in a laundry business and waitressing in a local restaurant. Collin knew what would have to come next. The only way out for the young May would be an early marriage, and that occurred immediately after May graduated from high school, at seventeen-years-of-age.

Collin leaned back and closed his eyes, thinking about May, how limited her choices were. He thought of his own daughter, how anxious he was to see her through school to a profession that challenged her and also provided stability for her. Now, she dribbled away her summer and there was nothing about it that he liked. At least May got out of high school. He needed to rest from that story, and so he watched the nurse collect her things and leave.

Julie started the laundry, and then settled down at May's desk to take care of the mail. Collin looked briefly at her back and then returned to reading more of the diaries, except he couldn't concentrate and he kept looking at her, watching her write checks with her left hand, and not complaining. She never complained about anything. She seemed to know he was looking at her.

"Interesting reading?" she asked.

"Hardship, hardship, hardship," he said. "Makes me appreciate every dollar I've ever had. Her father, a logger, died when she was young, and her mother had to work doing laundry and waiting tables to put food on the table."

"I read, or rather struggled through, bits and pieces of the diaries. I'm sorry I didn't start at the beginning. She probably married young, right?"

"Right."

"And to another logger."

"Right again. You're very smart. She married Harold Riley, a logger and another old time family."

"What I can be glad of, is that marriage lasted. Evidently."

"Change of topic. How's that working, paying bills using your left hand?"

"It's challenging, but worth it if I can avoid surgery. The pain's getting better. I think it's working."

"I think you're amazing. You do so much and so pleasantly." Who said that? Did he say that? He could have kicked himself. What had come over him? What will she say now? What will he say?

"Get back to reading," she said without turning around.

And he did, continuing on through delicate pages, faded ink, scrawled almost illegible handwriting, and tedious day-to-day entries about people, places, and things, but woven in were also the more dramatic days, the days of babies not coming to term, injuries from logging accidents, and her mother dying.

Collin did not go to sleep, but kept reading, engrossed in every detail, so much so that when Julie said, "What do you think of HH, do you think he's as nice as he appears?" He didn't respond, but kept reading, and let his mind work on all the details he was absorbing.

Chapter Twenty-Five

Andy, Tyler, and Sandy stood in the middle of the dark room -- gray floor, gray walls, and dirty windows. Boxes stacked on top of each other filled almost half of the room along with little chairs for little children stacked along one wall.

"We didn't know where to put all the stuff, so we cleaned out the smaller room next door and sort of carved out a space here in this big room and put the stuff over there. This door can be shut to make this a Sunday school room," said Tyler hopefully as he pointed to the flexible folded door that could be expanded across the room.

Andy surveyed the mess. How long had he been storing stuff in here, and telling everyone else to store stuff in here, and now they had to deal with the mess. One never escapes mess. "Sure appreciate you both taking on this project. Especially since I can't pay you."

Sandy shrugged. "Don't have another paying job for a couple of days."

"What we need, is for you to move all these boxes and chairs into the fellowship hall. That way we can thoroughly clean both rooms, paint them both, and use both spaces." He left.

Sandy and Tyler looked at each other. "I guess that's what we'll do," said Tyler. He moved the hand truck to the nearest stack of boxes and tried to lift the first box onto the truck. Sandy watched as he awkwardly balanced the box on one arm, holding it in place with the stump. As he stood up the box slipped out of his arms and dumped on the floor, papers and books spilling everywhere. "Shit," said Tyler.

Sandy knelt down and started cleaning up the mess.

"Stop it! Will you stop it!" said Tyler.

She stopped and sat down on the floor, ready for a fight. "What is the matter with you?" she asked. "I'm tired of tiptoeing around you."

"I'm tired of being helped," he said.

"It's always all about you. I'm tired of walking on eggshells around you."

He said nothing. She said nothing. She picked up some of the papers and looked at them. "This stuff is awful," she said.

"What is it?"

She handed him the papers.

"These are old Sunday School papers, like boring fill-in the blank stuff, maybe twenty years old. It's crap," he said.

"Would you please knock it off with the language? We're in church!"

He got up and looked through several of the other boxes. "All this stuff is old and useless and ought to go to the dump instead of the

Love that House

fellowship hall."

She got up and looked quickly through as many boxes as she could reach. From one box Sandy pulled out a dirty sweater, then a pair of gloves with holes in the fingers. She looked at the rest of the contents and grimaced. "This was evidently the lost and found box. From years ago. Come on."

She started for the door and he followed her down the hall to the pastor's office.

"Can we talk to you?" asked Sandy. Andy pointed to the chairs in front of his desk. Sandy shook her head no and then spoke.

"Those boxes, they're full of junk. Old Sunday school papers that no one will ever use and old clothes that no one will ever wear. All that stuff needs to go in the dumpster. It needs to not clutter up the fellowship hall."

"No. I've got to go through that stuff before it leaves the building."

Tyler stood in front of the door and said, "Andy. You may know more about God than I do, but I know more about junk than you do. And I'm not letting you go in there and waste your time. And ours. We are going to dump that stuff in the dumpster."

Andy frowned at both of them "You're both driving a hard bargain. What do I get out of it?"

"Everything in there, old clothes, old papers, old hard art supplies, is nothing you want to have around a kid now. We will let you know if we find anything else." Sandy gave Andy her most direct look, and then nodded to Tyler that they needed to leave.

*****

Going through each box, searching for anything that might be useful took time, Sandy and Tyler found little was worth keeping—one box containing children's scissors, a stapler, and seven children's Bibles was all that survived. Sandy and Tyler, exhausted, their backs aching, lay down on the floor to rest and congratulate themselves on a job well done. "We did good," said Tyler.

"I actually kind of like thinking about lots of little kids using these rooms, and learning about Jesus," said Sandy.

"Yeah," said Tyler as he got up, stretched, and looked at the stacked chairs.. "Lots of these chairs need some work. They're pretty rickety," said Tyler. He moved some of the chairs so that he could open the closet door. He found the light switch and walked in. Sandy heard him move more boxes. "Uh oh," he said.

"What's the matter?" asked Sandy.

"Come here."

Sandy peered cautiously into the closet.

"Look at this box of junk."

Sandy looked. "So? Looks like what we've been throwing out."

He took her hand, placed it on the box. Damp. "Oh no," she said.

"That's right. And look here," He pointed to the wall and then up to the ceiling. "A roof leak. It's a big uh-oh." Tyler moved the boxes out of the way and felt the floor of the closet.

"Well?" asked Sandy.

"Damp. Pastor Andy isn't going to be happy."

"Is it expensive to fix something like this?" asked Sandy.

"Yes. We're talking about replacing the roof probably. That'll be thousands of dollars. And this floor. I have no idea. It can't be cheap."

"Do you want to go tell him? I don't want to," asked Sandy.

"I don't want to, but I don't want you to either. Let's do it. Together. Now."

"Okay. Not only are we not making any money today, but you and I are about to tell our client he's got a big expensive problem. I'm not wild about this."

*****

Money. Never enough. Andy looked at the bills scattered on his desk and lifted his hands up. "Lord, I praise you, I thank you for your many blessings, for your son, and in his name I most humbly pray, that you would send this church a person to help with the finances, the bills of this church. I am not so good at organizing the money part of this church." He continued the conversation with God with his head in his hands, a conversation acknowledging not only his lack of money management skills, but his lack of patience, his envy of other people and what they owned and had in the bank. He acknowledged his exasperation with how motionless and self-concerned most of his parishioners were, and how he needed some new blood to infuse the church. And he hated the money problems. And now. A new roof.

*****

HH smiled big at Andy, but inside, HH's brain moved fast. *The pastor's here in my office and he is either concerned with my soul or money.* If it was his soul -- it would be easier. But, not to be.

"So, my finance manager moved out of the area, we need a new roof, and I was wondering if you could help."

And why not ask him, thought HH. Successful stockbroker, successful in New York City -- why not ask him? But, he was broke, and nobody knew it, even his wife and daughter, and no one must know it. He must find that painting, get his hands on it and get back on his feet. What was he to do with this pastor? Write him a check? Right now? And have the humiliation of the check bouncing? His ruse to get May and

Love that House

Julie out of the house so that he could search for the painting didn't work. Not only did they not leave, but that darn daughter of Collin's, Sandy, had moved in with May and Julie. Couldn't be a worse backfire, and now Collin, instead of going to Alaska, protected May, Julie, and Sandy with his overweight presence next door. HH took a deep breath.

"I will make you an offer," he said, smiling broadly again. "For every dollar you raise for the new church roof, I'll match it one hundred percent."

"Wow," said Andy. "That is more than generous."

"I'd like to help you out organizing the church finances, but I don't have time right now. This is what I can do."

"That's a huge help. I'll start fund-raising right away. Bless you."

Don't hurry. Do not hurry. Not until I get my hands on that house, or the painting, or both. I need to talk to that sleazy Van, or Fran. What does she know? What does she know about this pastor? He knows everything and is just trying to draw him out. Blackmail. The pastor is sitting right in front of me and acting innocent, when maybe he knows everything and trying to put the squeeze on me. I need that painting. Good, the pastor is leaving. Be gracious, get him out of the office and call Fran.

HH picked up the phone and barked at Fran as soon as she answered. "Can you talk?"

"Don't yell at me. Yes I can."

"I need to know what that pastor and/or Collin Matthews know about the painting, its history, and the value."

"Look. As far as I can tell, neither one of them knows anything. They think it's all about the house. And a few antiques, including the antique dollhouse. I don't think you have anything to worry about."

"Dammit, Fran..." Click. She hung up. He dialed her back.

"HH, don't ever talk to me like that or I will hang up again."

He sucked in his breath. He hated her. "Fran, I need more certainty than that. I need plan B, and to do plan B, I need to know for certain that neither one of them knows about the painting or its value. And you are part of this deal, it was what you said you could do. You are, after all, a woman, these are two bachelors. You were expected to work this out."

"HH, they are both a little harder to connect with than I thought."

"Fran, you're an attractive woman. They are men. Come on."

"HH. I'm telling you that I tried, but it didn't work. In the end, they both shied away from me. Quite frankly they didn't want what I had to give, and I have no indication that either of them knows about the painting, but my plan got stopped and that's all I know."

So, the pastor and Collin couldn't be bought or manipulated. At least not by Fran. That complicated things. Now he had to deal with that twerp, Van. So be it.

Chapter Twenty-Six

Julie loved feeling the fresh air on her face as she walked briskly toward the church, watching the ferry pull out and waving at now familiar faces. She needed this outing away from May, who continued to hang on to life with remarkable tenacity. When Pastor Andy made it clear he needed her artistic talent, she agreed without hesitation.

Inside the church she found him looking at the room the kids had cleaned out. "They did a good job," she said.

"They did. And I'm glad they found the roof leak before the damage became catastrophic."

"You didn't get up there and fix it, did you?"

"I'm a pastor and that means I can do many things. So, what do you think? I'd like for this room to be cheerful and for kids to want to be here. What would you suggest?"

"I'm catching on to what you're about. I see glimpses of what Christ is about. And I get it that you want this room to reflect that for little kids."

"Did you go to Sunday School when you were a kid?" he asked.

"Yes, I did. And I feel like a kid again. My renewed interest in Christ -- it's like it's all new, and rather exciting. People think it's a hardship on me, to come up here and take care of May and put my career on hold, but honestly, I can't wait to get up early in the morning, before the sun comes up, and read May's Bible. A joy is coming back in my life."

She didn't dare look at him. In the brief talks they had shared over the past weeks, he never pushed her, always answered her questions, and always encouraged her. Absentmindedly, she moved to a book left on the windowsill and picked it up, revealing a dead mouse in back of it. "Oh!" she said and jumped back. She laughed at herself while Andy picked it up and took it outside.

"What age group will use this room?" she asked when he returned.

"I'm thinking I'll put the middle schoolers in here. That's a difficult age group and I really don't know how to decorate a room for them. They are generally deep into our culture, unfortunately, and not that interested in the bright colors and simple decorations the younger kids like."

"Yes, it's easier to think about a room for the younger kids." She wandered around, looking at the light and thinking, when the church secretary burst into the room.

"Steve, Mabel's son called. Mabel's missing. They're combing the town looking for her."

*****

Andy didn't hurry. He finished talking with Julie and talked to God. He knew the family was concerned and the town itself was big enough to take some time looking for an old person, and, for sure, you wouldn't want an elderly person wandering off into the forest. Once a person started into the forest, a bad story could develop rapidly. Tall, thick trees, no sunlight, wild animals -- it would be easy for anybody to get disoriented and get lost. But that wasn't really on his mind. He knew Mabel better than that.

Andy walked between the cars waiting to get on the ferry. When he got to the terminal and the waiting area for walk-on passengers, he looked around at the diverse group of people but he did not see Mabel. He still wasn't worried and he stood at the back and waited, and soon she emerged from the restroom and sat down near a window. Tiny little thing, full of trouble. Andy sat down beside her, smiling into her terror-stricken face.

"Don't make me go back. I don't want the medical treatment, I don't want to be with my family. Those kids are nuts. I want to go home and die." She lifted her chin defiantly.

"Are you kidding me? You don't love your grandchildren? You don't want to spend time with them and go to their basketball games and see them get married?"

"They're rude, they don't care about me, they don't play basketball, and I think they're worthless. I want to go back to the island."

"To do what?"

"To die."

He nodded. "I think you've got that about right. You're in a bad way. Are you sure you don't want to be here with your family, walk with them through possible treatment and dying?"

She shook her head.

"Do you think you're being selfish?"

"It's my life. I've given a fair amount of my life for all of them. Why can't I go back to my cabin to hear the birds and spend my time with my own memories and die? I'll leave money for all of them, even after I've taken care of myself in my own cabin."

She watched him carefully but he said nothing. "See, you don't understand. You're on their side."

"Not at all," he said. "I'll make a deal with you. Let's get you back to your son's house. I'll go with you, and we will share all these ideas with him and his wife."

"Not those grandkids! They were cute when they were little, but now, they're just a pain."

"I think that's right. I can support that. This is mainly between you and Steve, his wife and me. Let's do that and share these ideas."

"Only if you're going to be on my side. If you aren't, I'm going to get on the ferry. Here it comes." She pressed her lips firmly together.

"Okay. I agree. I'll be your advocate. But you have to listen to everything they have to say. And be polite about it."

She nodded.

"Don't just nod at me, Mabel. Say you understand. Now."

"I understand. And I appreciate you taking this on. Probably uncomfortable for you."

"I can't believe it. You just showed a little interest in someone else. That's rare."

"Don't start with me, Pastor Andy. Don't start with me."

Before Andy could reply, Collin appeared.

"You already figured it out," said Collin as he stood above them. "I guess a pastor would. Actually took me a while. Going back to the island, Mabel?"

"Not today. She's going to talk to Steve and his wife about it and I said I would help her. Right now she's going back to Steve's house."

Collin picked up her bag, Andy helped her up, and the two men walked with her back to Collin's car

Chapter Twenty-Seven

Walking up the sidewalk, Collin admired the workmanship of the painters, and he was happy at the same time that he wouldn't have to pay the bill. The house, some would call beautiful, a Victorian thing of beige with black and green trim looked impressive. HH answered the bell and showed him into the living room, full of antiques and modern luxuries, including a fifty-three inch TV.

"Quite the house, and quite the upkeep!" said Collin.

"Yes, been in the family for several generations, but that's about to change."

"Really? You're going to sell it?"

"Yes. New York is now our home. Our only daughter is in college and the upkeep is expensive."

"You don't want that daughter to have this family legacy? Make a great summer home."

"No. I don't believe in spoiling kids. She will do fine without this house. We're going to have to let go of some family history and downsize. But enough of that. What brings you here today?"

"It's about May and Julie and yourself."

HH stiffened. "What do you mean?"

"What I mean is this. Julie's work has been taking care of May at the expense of her own work, and since it seems almost certain that May's estate, in other words, the house, will go to the two of you, I wanted to suggest something."

"Let me guess. Since I am the successful New York stockbroker, you think Julie should have the house?"

"Julie's been pretty busy taking care of May, for about two months now. But I have another thought."

HH creased his lips into what might be considered a smile. "I'm listening."

"Since you are in to antiques, I wonder if there couldn't be a split -- you would take the contents of the house, all those miniatures and antiques, and that Julie could have clear title to the house."

"You've taken quite an interest in her, haven't you?"

Collin didn't respond.

HH waited on Collin, but he thought it was a great idea. The painting had to be in the house. It had to be. If Collin knew about the painting, he would never negotiate away the possession of the contents of the house. This was a deal made for HH. But he needed to play it cool.

"I don't know. That's a valuable piece of property."

"Of course that's true, but you're a successful man with so much, and I don't think the insides of the house are trivial."

"So, wealth isn't a bad thing in your mind?" asked HH.

"Not at all. I've done a fair amount of wealth building myself and wouldn't mind more. So, no, I'm not into taking from you and giving to Julie, not at all. I'm thinking May has been shrewd all these years, and you would not be disappointed. I took the liberty of researching just two of the prints May has on her walls, and if the names Dross and Gould mean anything to you, then that's only a start on what she has in there."

This Collin's was a smart businessman. He owned the house next door and was probably interested in Julie and her house being a part of the deal. But what did he care, really? Without any hassle at all, Collin just offered him exactly what he wanted. The painting. It had to be there. Jared James must have taken it there the morning he died and supposedly was delivering food.

"Collin. You are so right. I have so much. I appreciate Julie and what she does. I would want her to have the little house and sure, I'll seriously consider letting go of any claim to the house itself in exchange for its contents."

*****

"Let's have a dinner, a fund-raising dinner in a few weeks, and get enough money to fix this roof and the new Sunday school room," said Collin as he looked at the roof. "I think the whole roof needs to be replaced."

"Come on down. You're too old to be up there," said Andy.

"Just a minute. I'm going to check over the whole thing." He walked over both sides of the roof covering the classrooms and fellowship center, and then he walked the roof covering the offices, and then the sanctuary. Andy stood back and watched, more than irritated.

"You know we've done that already. Do you think you're more insightful about the roof than the rest of us?"

Finally, Collin climbed down the ladder.

"Anything new?" asked Andy.

"No I guess not. I just like to see things for myself."

"So, Julie says she's going to help me figure out paint colors and decorations for the classrooms."

"Really? I didn't know she had been around. She taking an interest in your church?"

"Come on, Collin. I don't talk about people and their spiritual walks in life. You know that wouldn't be right."

"Sure." But Collin was still curious about Andy's possible interest in her.

"By the way. You've got a good idea for a fundraiser. HH said he would do a match -- any money we raised for the roof he would match one hundred percent."

Collin didn't like that. He could have done the same thing. Now he had to be publicly even more appreciative of HH. All of it pushed Collin to the limits of his patience, but he knew he needed to let the man be the hero. Still, Collin didn't like it.

"I had a talk with HH myself, today."

"Anything you can share with me?" asked Andy.

"Sure. I have no pastoral constraints. I convinced him to agree, at least with me in private, to let Julie have the house. If May has left all of her worldly goods to be split between Julie and HH, then HH has said to me he would step aside about the house."

"No kidding. In exchange for what?"

"In exchange for the contents of the house. She was quite an antique collector."

"Hard to believe the contents could be equal to the value of the cottage with that view on the bluff," said Andy.

"Antiques and art -- many people's passion and they pay big for such."

Andy said, "I've got to get back to my office."

Sure you do, thought Collin. *I just trumped you.*

"Any word about Mabel?" asked Collin.

"She came to a compromise with her family. She'll get her health tests done this week, have an evaluation with her doctors, and then if she wants to go back to the island to die, they said they would support her decision."

Collin thought about that and then asked, "Are you going to be a part of any of those discussions?"

"I told the family I would support whatever they decide. But if she goes back, they have to take her. Not me. And not you."

"Good. Thanks for leaving me out. Sometimes I think you have a soft job, and then sometimes I think it must be really hard."

Andy waved at him and reentered the church.

*****

"Oh, no," said Collin. He rubbed his eyes and then pressed his hand against them.

Julie looked at him. Is he weeping? She took the diary out of his hands to see what had Collin so upset. The passage simply read: *Harold, Harold. How could you leave me?*

That was all that marked the day Harold died. Julie couldn't force herself to read further. She put the diary down. Collin, the ever stoic, ever doing something, had put his hands over his face. He was, indeed, weeping. Should she get up and put an arm around him? There lay May, so very close now to the end of her life, and here sat Collin, very much alive and weeping now as if a dam had broken. Julie sat very still, aware of both of them, rain on the roof and a clock ticking.

The front door opened. Sandy, startled, looked at her dad and stopped at the door. Julie walked over to her and smiled uncertainly.

"Why is Dad crying? Did May die?" Sandy whispered.

"No."

"I've got to get back to work. I needed my rain jacket," said Sandy. She quickly glanced at her dad, grabbed her jacket and left.

Collin continued weeping, lost in his own world of grief. Julie went to the kitchen, fixed a cup of tea and returned to sit closer to him. Death was almost here, she was tired, and Collin's sorrow filled any remaining places in her soul this day. Should she hand him a tissue? He took care of that, pulling a white handkerchief out of his pocket, blowing his nose noisily, and then leaning back against the couch, staring at the ceiling.

"Do you realize how little I cried when Jan died? And now, it seems almost anything triggers a waterfall," he said.

"I didn't realize that. It's been what, a year and a half? That's a long time to avoid pain."

"You know, I can't imagine living May's life. I almost can't bear it. How hard they worked, logging and farming, and then to lose it all. And then she loses him."

"I can hardly wait to find what happens after that. This is better than a TV reality show. Sort of like reading a book backwards, or watching a reality TV show backwards, isn't it?"

Collin didn't answer her; he thought about how vulnerable she was and what he knew would have to wait, except she would probably keep asking questions.

"So how did she end up with this primo property?" asked Julie.

Collin took his time answering. "Well, her brother, the original HH, out of the goodness of his heart, saved her by buying her property and setting her up here."

"Sounds like he was a loving brother," said Julie. "Maybe it's appropriate that this property end up back in his grandson's hands."

"You're pretty generous, especially when it could also end up in your hands."

"We'll see. What I know is I've benefited from being here. I'm more optimistic that my wrist is healing. I'm almost ready to go back to my life."

"You might want to remember that while this property is extremely valuable now, back then it was considered less than great. Back then, the harbor was noisy, dirty, and this whole neighborhood was considered lower class. But, she did have a place to live, and she worked some at the library, when her health permitted, and of course she volunteered at her church, until she couldn't do either anymore."

Collin waited, hoping she would move off the subject.

"They didn't even have any kids. At least you had Sandy after Jan died. That has to be a great source of comfort," said Julie.

"I can't imagine not having her, although I'm pretty clumsy at fatherhood."

"I don't have any kids. Maybe I should get a cat. You're lucky to have Sandy, and she does need you."

"I really haven't been a very good father. And she knows that. She has every reason to hate me -- instead she wanted to spend this summer with me. Even after I basically abandoned her after Jan died. Before Jan died, actually. How can I possibly make that up to her? Now, she's hanging around with Tyler, and I almost abandoned her again this summer by going to Alaska. Some dad."

Julie bent over May, gently stroking her face. She tucked the blankets around May's shoulders before returning to where Collin was seated, and then sat back down with her hands in her lap. "Collin, I need to ask you something."

"Sure. What?"

"What was Jan like?"

He grimaced. "I don't think I can talk about her. I just can't. I will say this, she was beautiful, smart, and very very patient. She put up with more than she should have from me. But, that's probably all I can say."

"That's okay. I understand."

"I'm not sure you do. You see, I feel guilty -- I took her for granted. I can hardly talk about her now because she seems so wonderful, and I didn't appreciate her then. It seems unconscionable to even mention her name. She deserved better. She deserved better than me, and I wish I could live my life over again. I'm a sorry bloke."

*****

Collin and Julie left May in the living room and moved to the kitchen where they quietly drank coffee and surveyed the busy scene below them.

"Lots of busyness down there," said Collin. "I wonder if people will find it meaningful next week, next month, or next year."

"Pastor Andy has helped me a lot to see through the busyness and see more of God."

"Andy's a wise man in many ways. I don't see how he does it. He never had a family, never built a business. I'm starting to respect him. I'm still not plugging in on being the kind of Christian he talks about."

Julie smiled. "I don't think he would mind me telling you this. That he almost had a family. His fiancée died right before they were to get married, right before he graduated from seminary."

Collin face fell and he felt his insides sink. "That's terrible. And I've been beating him up with words every chance I can get. Over and over,

I've let him know he's not lived a real life with any real pain. What a dumbass I've been."

Collin didn't say it out loud, but he also thought about how Julie often quoted Andy. She was getting wisdom from Andy, which was more than she was getting from him. While he was busy running around, trying to overtly help people, and yes, get accolades for himself, Andy was quietly proving himself indispensable.

"Are you a Christian?" asked Collin.

"I accepted Christ years ago," said Julie. "But, my support group and some counseling really got me on track. Taught me about openness, facing life on life's terms, and real day to day help. But it's only since I've been here, working with May, getting to know people, including Andy, that I've started thinking that being a Christian is a real path. A path to walk daily. Christ is slowly becoming more real. I'll never give up my support group, though. Does that answer your question?"

Well, that Andy knew how to make inroads with the woman that he himself was interested in. Andy could have had Fran. Collin practically gave him Fran, but he didn't want her. Now they were both interested in the same woman, and Andy had been sneakily making progress which apparently was leaving Collin behind and scrambling. There was only one thing to do. "That Andy is quite a guy," said Collin. That was good, a space-saver in the conversation until he could do better.

"You've given a lot of your time here, and it's been stressful on your career," said Collin. Now was not the time to tell her that he also had been busy on her behalf, and by getting HH to at least verbally agree that Julie deserved the house, he had contributed a great deal to Julie's well-being. That would come out later.

"It's been a real surrendering," said Julie.

"I don't surrender to anybody or anything," said Collin.

She laughed gently. "I used to be able to say that. With pride -- but I had to -- there was no other place to go. I had to just give up and count on something other than myself."

"God?"

"Yes, God as my source, rather than my well-meaning willpower. I could not be doing this, have any graciousness with May or anyone else if it were not for that."

"It's hard to imagine you being different from what I see now."

"Trust me. I can and have snapped the heads off any and every one that I know."

"Actually, I do remember what you were like when you first arrived. I thought you were cranky because of your arm and everything. Reason enough to be angry at the world."

"Maybe so, but I can see that I was like that pretty much all the time for any reason. Another thing Andy and I've talked about is I've made some business deals that I'm not real proud of."

Collin's eyes opened wider. "You? Really?"

"Yes. I can talk to Andy about anything."

"Like, what do you mean? Are you afraid you're going to hell because of some bad decisions?"

"Not at all. I see God's forgiveness. I see God's strength. I see more clearly what his son, Jesus, was about."

May's breathing grew louder as she struggled for air. Julie motioned for Collin to join her, and they each sat on either side of May. She and Collin held hands and each also rested a hand on May, and with Julie saying the Lord's Prayer, May passed on.

Collin sat very still with his eyes closed. He opened his eyes when he felt Julie slowly withdraw her hand. Julie went to the phone. He lightly stroked May's head and then he left.

Chapter Twenty-Eight

"I don't know what I did before this," said Julie, looking at the bed May had recently occupied. "It's like this has been my whole life. Forever."

"No doubt your friends in New Mexico miss you," said Andy as he stripped the bed.

"Friends? New Mexico? Seems so far away. I don't quite believe it's over."

Andy took the linens to the hallway and dumped them on the washing machine. Collin watched, wishing he had thought to do that.

"Since she no longer has a connection with a church, HH has said he doesn't care what kind of service, if any -- looks like it's up to you," Andy said to Julie.

She smiled and shrugged. "I don't know what's appropriate. She didn't even leave a request about what to do with her ashes."

"I have a suggestion," said Collin. "Let's take her ashes out on my boat, in the middle of the Strait, and spread her ashes there. She loved sitting out there on her deck, looking at the harbor traffic and the strait."

"What do you think?" asked Andy as he looked at Julie.

She nodded. "I think we still need to have a party. There are people here in town who knew her, and to not have a celebration of her life would be a shame."

Collin stood up. Energized, seeing another path for himself, he said, "Let's have a party out in front of my house, underneath the trees. I'll provide the food. People can drop by. It will be a great thing." He looked at both of them hopefully.

"Sounds like a plan to me," said Andy. They both turned to Julie. She nodded, and added, "But, it needs to be a potluck. That will make it more fun."

*****

Collin wanted to provide the perfect spiritual experience. His boat, a beautiful day of sailing, the wind filling the sails, small white caps on the water, the sun on their faces. He envisioned Andy saying something proper and appropriate, and they would then spread the ashes in the water, and a peace that defied anything any of them had ever felt before would fill their souls, fill them with a quiet that they would remember the rest of their lives. On his boat.

They did not put the sails up because there was almost no wind. The diesel throbbed away as they pushed into the strait, and with just a little bit of choppy water, the boat rocked up and down, not dangerously, but a rocking motion that was ceaseless and demanding in its own way. Demanding enough that Collin noticed Andy looked green and grim. Julie was afraid to stand up, because of the rocking. She smiled tentatively at Collin as the boat moved forward, up and down, up and down. A large oil tanker passed in front of them and Collin knew that once the wake reached them, Andy would turn even greener.

"When do we spread the ashes?" Collin yelled at them above the sound of the engine. "Anytime is fine with me," said Julie. Andy nodded.

"Do you have something to say?" asked Collin, knowing it was big of him to want Andy to look good. Andy opened his mouth, shut it, and then leaned over the side of the boat, losing whatever he had for breakfast. Collin rushed to him, afraid Andy might pitch himself over, but Julie beat him to it. Julie, held his belt until Andy was finally through. Andy sat back down, looking exhausted. Collin handed him the ashes, a box meant to dissolve in the water. Andy gently placed it in the water, and without a word, the three of them watched the box slowly melt into the water.

*****

The next order of business, and Julie was adamant this occur before settling the business of May's estate, would be a celebration of May's life. The challenge, of course, was that no one actually knew her, since she had out-lived most of her peers, and had dropped out of her church activities some years before. Collin knew her better than anybody, and he was going to make the most of that chance to look good -- an opportunity to be magnanimous should not be missed.

A gathering of neighbors and townspeople, underneath his own magnificent maple trees, with fresh lemonade, laughing children, people sharing food and stories, some, at least, would be about May. Andy loaned him long tables and chairs from the church, and Tyler delivered them, stacking them against the two old maple trees. The partly cloudy sky lent itself to an outdoor gathering thought Collin, and then he remembered the cameras. He needed to get the security cameras down and change the flash drives before he had hundreds of boring pictures of the neighbors on his lawn.

Collin took the camera off the post in his backyard, opened it, took the flash drive out, put a new one in, and then repeated the process with the camera from the tree in his front yard.

Officer Howard walked by, saw what Collin was doing, and stopped. "Camera's been working okay?"

"Sure. I don't even need to see the pictures. People just knowing the cameras are here works fine. I don't even lock my doors."

"It's a changing town," said Howard. "The drugs and God only knows what coming in. I'm amazed you leave your doors unlocked."

"Sort of a dream I want to live, I guess. Small town, people trusting each other. Jan dreamed of it for both of us."

"She must have been a fine woman. You lost her early." Officer Howard leaned against the tree like he was tired, but his face reflected alertness and compassion.

Collin nodded. He felt weepy again but didn't want it to show. "I'm going to put these up around May's house."

"You really think these cameras are necessary? May's gone, the drugs are gone. Not much but knickknacks in her house. Old people tend to do that. Not even a modern TV."

"I know. Just a precaution. Until Julie leaves town."

Collin placed a camera in the back, focused on the back door of May's house, and then he retrieved a third camera from inside his house and put it on the side of May's house in the bushes where the break-in occurred. Collin was tying the final camera to the fir tree in May's front yard, with it aimed at the front of the house, when a car pulled up and stopped. HH got out and started up the sidewalk carrying a large box.

"Good morning, Collin. My lovely wife made a cake for the afternoon's event, thought I would bring it by early." He smiled broadly at Collin and looked with interest at the camera.

"If I hadn't seen you place it there, I wouldn't know it was there," he said.

"Yeah, they make these cameras so they blend in with the environment. Don't have to hide it."

"That's good you're doing that. I'm glad you're doing it."

"Good protection, for the house, for Julie, for yourself."

"I appreciate it and I want you to know I've been thinking about what we talked about, and if I have a chance, I'm pretty interested in being generous with Julie. She's done a fine job here, and I appreciate it. I, as you have said, have much to be grateful for."

"Wonderful," said Collin, as he stepped away from the tree and looked critically at the camera before he turned to HH. "An expert like you could no doubt do quite well with the contents of a house like this."

Julie came out, drying her hands on a towel, and smiling at HH. "Marileta has been baking, hasn't she?"

"She has indeed. And I need to get going before Collin here asks me to help set up tables. I'm not used to actual work." He handed her the box, nodded to both of them. "I've also got company. An art dealer from Stillwater Harbor. Collin's met her."

"Are you talking about Fran?"

"Yes. Lovely lady, isn't she? I must go." He turned and left.

"I like your camera idea. At least if somebody messes with this house, you'll have faces to question," said Julie.

"Do you think it's going to rain?" he asked.

"It isn't supposed to. I'll help you set up the tables and chairs. I have time right now."

Collin frowned. "Tyler was supposed to come back and help me. He said he was coming right back."

Julie threw the towel on the porch and smiled brightly. "Let's do it. When he shows up, I'm sure you'll find something else for him to do." She marched over to his house with a vigor he wished he saw in Tyler. He ran to keep up with her. "Sandy's been much bossier lately, and I know where she's getting it. You're one determined woman."

*****

Collin watched from his porch as the rain pelted the tables and chairs he and Julie had set up. Pools of water developed in the seats of the chairs. Sandy ran across the yard and stood beside him, silently watching the rain.

"What's Julie doing?" asked Collin.

"Same thing we are. Watching this from the window. I don't think it's going to stop anytime soon," said Sandy.

"I'm going to volunteer to drive her to the lawyer's office tomorrow and I've got an idea for another kind of memorial dinner," said Collin. He took Sandy's umbrella from her and ran across the lawn. As he shook the rain off the umbrella, Julie stepped outside.

"It seems to me that one little old lady should have a quiet celebration of her life, even if hardly anyone remembers her. Can you believe this rain? Do you want some coffee?" she asked.

"No. Not right now. But I've got an idea for another kind of service. I'll invite Van, Andy, HH, and that art dealer, Fran, all of them to dinner tonight here. And Tyler and Sandy. We'll get rid of some of the food and have a little talk. Honoring May."

"That doesn't sound very promising to me, but Andy will make it interesting," said Julie.

Andy would make it interesting? Julie wanted interesting? He would make it an evening that none of them would forget.

*****

Collin found Van in Jared James' office. "Van, come on by May's house tonight, after work, about six o'clock. Several of us are going to have a small dinner commemorating May's life." Collin didn't make it an invitation, but a command, and Van looked at him skeptically.

"Don't think I can, but thanks for thinking of me. I didn't actually know her that well."

Stepping closer, Collin said, "Really? I've got a great picture of you, from my wildlife camera, running across my yard, while I was in Alaska.

Dated by the camera the same night of the attempted break-in at May's house. I'm pretty sure it's you."

"You're nuts. What are you talking about? I know for a fact that you only put up those cameras today. What are you trying to pull?"

"The cameras have been in my yard, and I just changed them to May's yard. Show up tonight and we'll talk about it."

Collin turned and headed for the church and Andy, and he had the same imperative statement for Andy.

"What do you want me there for?" asked Andy. "If you're trying to make me a peacemaker between the two heirs, I don't want to be there. Not my kind of business."

"Fran is going to be there. She likes you. So does Julie. Be there."

*****

HH sat at his desk, looking at the bills, looking at the bank statements, all the while hearing the voices in his mind of the people who had loaned him money and now wanted repayment. Marileta sat across from him knitting, talking nonstop about their daughter, the neighbors, and how glad she would be to get back to New York. Keeping everything a secret from Marileta was not hard, because she kept her eyes closed to everything that didn't interest her. Plus, she had absolute faith in her husband. Marileta had no idea how far in debt they were or who they were in debt to, and even if he told her, she would brush it off with her eternal optimism. They were both so locked into their own minds and thoughts that they both jumped when they heard loud pounding on the front door, someone entered and slammed the door shut before either could get up, and then there was Collin, breathing heavily, standing in front of them, drenched from the rain.

"What do you think you're doing?" said HH.

"Inviting you and your wife to dinner at May's house. Tonight."

"Kind of sudden, isn't it?"

"*No*. You need to be there, your wife's attendance is optional. The rain will continue, so our outdoor celebration is canceled, but tonight we will have a dinner with a few select guests."

"You're awfully demanding when it comes to me and my wife," said HH, moving to stand in front of Collin, but Collin didn't move.

"It's in your best interest to be there."

Marileta's mouth dropped open. Her gaze trailed after Collin as he left and then she stared at her husband.

"Don't worry about it," HH said. "You'll stay home but I'll go. Nothing for you to concern yourself with."

Marileta smiled hesitantly at him and then resumed knitting. "I know you'll take care of it."

*****

Collin bounded down the steps and almost ran into Tyler on his bicycle. "Weren't you supposed to help this afternoon with the tables at May's house?"

"Yeah, sure, but it was raining, and I had something else I needed to do."

Collin grabbed him by the collar and drew the young man close to him. "You needed to come by anyway or at least call. What's the matter with you? I think you are the most spoiled kid I've met in a long time. You get away with way too much." He let go of Tyler's collar and glared at him.

"You, Collin, you just can't stand your daughter hanging out with me, a guy without two good arms."

Collin again grabbed Tyler by the collar and pushed him backwards against a tree. "You are a half-baked slime ball if you really think that."

Tyler, frozen, didn't say a word. Collin gave him the same directive that he gave the others and then left, storming down the sidewalk with the energy of a man used to getting his own way. Collin was tired of them all, tired of their smallness, and tired of his own mind, which had been half alive ever since Jan died. Half alive, taking half steps, and absorbing way too much from other people. He would clear the air, clear his mind, and still have the rest of the summer for sailing and writing.

Chapter Twenty-Nine

The gathering at May's house was much like a family Christmas dinner where everyone knew they were supposed to have a good time, but each was actually waiting for the usual barbs from one another. The goal, of course, was then to deliver the best zinger, collect the best leftovers to take home, and then leave.

The pies, baked chicken, green salad, and bread given by the neighbors filled the counter in May's kitchen. Each attendee filled his or her own plate and found a place to sit in the living room.

Everyone took time to compliment Julie on the care she provided May, and all struggled to come up with valid memories of May. Collin, quietly in the background, amiable and smiling, enjoyed the unease that he had helped create.

By the time Julie cleared away the dishes, including the wine glasses -- one glass of wine being allotted to each guest -- the conversation was over. Collin, however, wanted them to squirm a little more. He wanted to see what would happen next. More awkward small talk? Let the tension build.

Fran was the first to try and escape the uneasy feel that persisted through the evening. She smiled at everyone, and then said, "This has been lovely, a lovely remembrance of a lovely woman, in this lovely little town. But I actually must leave so that I can make the late ferry back home. Work! Work! Work!"

Collin stood up. "Before you go, I'd like to address an issue about the celebration tonight while we are all together." All heads faced him, faces frozen. "I'd like to address the issue of Jared James' death."

HH spoke first. "Oh, Collin, that was long ago and what is the point?"

"The point is this. May kept diaries, detailed diaries from when she was a young girl until just a few weeks ago, when she became unable to write."

"Where are these diaries?" asked HH. "I want to see them for myself."

"I've got them in a safe place. But I am about to tell you some things I learned from them, that all of you will find interesting."

Fran settled back into her chair.

"Decades ago, May and her husband, who had few financial resources, got married, worked hard, and made a down payment on a farm about 20 miles south of here. They thought they could make a good future for themselves, and one of the reasons was they had a very valuable miniature painting in their possession. A tiny miniature painting by a famous artist, Bierstadt. One of those things artists painted and gave away as they traveled around exploring the West in the 1800s. Traveling artists paid their room and board with these paintings. That painting was originally given to Harold's great grandparents and passed down to him. Now, this painting is worth a fortune."

Collin looked at Fran. "Accurate?"

Fran shrugged, unable to talk.

HH stood up. "None of this is important. I'm leaving."

"Sit down, HH. Now. Or I call the police."

HH sat down and no one else made a sound.

"Let's go on with the diaries. Harold, unfortunately died young from a logging accident, and May was faced with some decisions. And her big brother, HH I, helped her. He bought the farm from her, which got her out from under the mortgage, and took the painting, telling her he would sell it for her in New York."

"I think it sounds like the big brother did right by her. She ended up here in this sweet cottage, and with some part time jobs, had a pleasant life," said Andy.

"The thing about May's diaries is that not only did she record her life and thoughts, but she also included old clippings. She included a clipping about the railroad buying property at a premium price for the line built south of here -- HH the first made a bundle on the property he bought at a discount from May when her husband died."

That left everyone speechless. Collin kept on.

"You're probably wondering about the little painting?" asked Collin. He looked at HH.

"I've heard of it," said HH.

"Sure you have, because your grandfather took it from his sister."

"That's not right, she gave it to him to sell in New York for her!" said HH.

The group looked at him and then back at Collin. Collin smiled.

"That's right. Very good, HH. But the thing is he told May he would sell it for her when the market was right, but he never did. He always claimed the market wasn't right."

"So where is the painting?" asked Sandy.

"According to May's diaries, her brother always brushed her off when she asked about the painting. But she wrote in her diaries, the following, which several people relayed to her as rumors, that HH the second, had an affair many years ago, and Jared James's father blackmailed him, told him he would tell the whole town, unless HH II gave him the painting, and that's what HH the II did. He gave the painting to Jared James' father to put in the Victorian dollhouse, and the senior Mr. James always kept his mouth shut. Mr. James was obsessed with the dollhouse and the miniatures in it, happy to have the painting for his personal enjoyment, and so was his son, Jared James."

"Now wait a minute," said Andy. "If nobody talked, where did the rumors come from?"

"I don't know," said Collin. "And we'll likely never know."

"But the painting wasn't there. I checked! His daughter had me inventory everything in that dollhouse when he died, and it wasn't there!" said Van.

"So, where is the painting now?" asked Sandy.

"I think HH and Van and Fran have already figured that out," said Collin. "And by reading the diaries, I've figured it out, too. It's in this house. Jared James likely brought it back here, after May had her stroke, and put it in this house for safe-keeping, the morning he brought food for the dinner he and Julie planned to have later that day."

"How could you know that?" asked Tyler.

"I don't know that, but she wrote in her diary that she was wary of Jared hanging around those last few weeks, before her stroke, and she figured he was feeling guilty in his old age. So, if he was, I figure he wanted to give it back to her, but since she had a stroke, and in his mind, would die before he did, he wanted to return it to her, or at least this house, and assuage his own guilt."

Every person looked around, wondering what the little painting would look like and where it would be.

"Don't worry, I'm pretty sure I know where it is, but the question is, who should go home with it?"

Julie threw up her hands in disgust. "I'm sick of this whole disgusting story. This poor woman needed a break in life and she didn't get it."

"Since it comes down to you and HH as heirs, would you let him have the painting and the contents of this house in exchange for you getting title to the house?"

"Sure. Anything for all this to be over and I can go on with my life."

"I would say, in front of all these witnesses, that if I could walk out of here with the painting, I will relinquish all rights to the house, the contents, and anything else of May's," said HH.

All eyes riveted to Julie and she nodded.

"Then come with me to May's sewing room," said Collin as he motioned to HH. "I'm almost certain that when Jared entered the house that morning, with no one to watch him, he pinned that painting up on that messy wall, the one covered with clippings, greeting cards, and whatever else, where it would be hidden and safe, returned to May and found by someone who would appreciate it."

"You're kidding? It's not in a safe? He hid it in plain view?" asked HH.

"You've got one hour to find it. Let's go, before I get impatient and call the sheriff."

HH hustled into the sewing room with Collin. Collin watched HH immediately and carefully start taking down the items on the wall, looking each one over carefully and laying each one by one on the bed.

"Don't bother anything else, I don't want any other trouble from you. When you find it, say goodbye to everyone and leave. Or I'll make good on that threat of the sheriff, and tell him about Van being caught on my camera, and we will all start to wonder seriously about Jared James' brakes and who might have helped him have that so called accident."

HH nodded and kept working. Collin returned to the living room, looked at the quiet, slack-jawed people, and said cheerfully, "I could use another piece of pie."

*****

Collin stood in the living room by the door, eating his second piece of pie. The others watched him, unable to say anything, mesmerized by the situation and wondering what would happen next.

HH emerged from the hallway, smiling and buttoning his jacket.

"Get what you came for?" asked Collin.

"Indeed."

"That means you won't be back, you won't give Julie any trouble about anything, and all these people will make your life miserable if you don't keep your word. Correct?"

"Absolutely. I'm on my way."

"You can't just let him go!" said Tyler. "He probably killed my grandpa!"

HH froze and then said, "Are you still claiming Jared didn't die from an accident?"

"I'm saying someone probably tampered with his bicycle brakes and you had a reason to. You wanted that stupid painting and he wouldn't let you have it."

"Wait a minute," said Collin. "There are several people here that could have had an interest in getting the painting."

"Like who else?" asked Tyler.

"Maybe Andy."

"What?" asked Andy standing up, looking like he wanted to throw something.

"Sure. Andy needs money for the church, always, and so he learns about the painting from town gossip and decides it should be his. Or, Fran could have an obvious interest in the painting. Or so could Van. Van has been mistreated and unappreciated in this town, second in command at the local museum. Extra money could help."

"You're right, you are absolutely right," said Van as he stood up next to Andy, who quickly sat down again.

"Right about what?" asked Collin.

"I was sick and tired of being second; Jared James was a real control freak."

"So, probably HH or even Fran or even the good pastor Andy put you up to tampering with the brakes of that bicycle, a chance for some real money?" Collin continued to stand in front of the door so that no one could leave.

"You tell him the truth, or so help me you will regret it," said HH. "Tell him I had nothing to do with you and those brakes."

"Nor did I," said Andy.

"I had nothing to do with that," said Fran.

"It was her!" said Van, clenching his fists.

"What do you mean, her?" asked Collin, advancing to stand in front of Van.

"It was May. You don't believe me, do you? It was May. She had me over to her house once in a while, and we both vented about Jared. We both related with each other in our hatred of the self-centered weasel, and she never actually told me to do it. But she said, she would like to hurt him, just like his family had hurt her, and pay him back."

"So, you tampered with the brakes and caused his death after she had a stroke and was dying? Does this make sense?"

"I felt bad for her. I never could bring myself to do anything to hurt him, and I felt guilty. Her laying there in the hospital, and that was the one thing she wanted, revenge on Jared and I hadn't done it for her. I felt bad for her, and I knew if I did it, not really meaning to kill him, but if I got him banged up, she would know about it. She could still hear. She would know about it, and my conscience would be clear."

"This is the most twisted example of greed, revenge, and unresolved issues I have ever personally had to deal with," said Andy. "I'm going home." He walked around Collin and HH and left.

"The rest of you, leave," said Collin.

HH followed Andy, and the rest of the group slowly filed out, leaving Julie and Collin looking at each other.

"You okay?" asked Collin.

"I can't get my arms around what just happened," said Julie. "The awfulness of all this, and I have been here taking care of this woman, who was in no way innocent in all this. It's just too much to handle right now. And I never did get to see the painting."

"What exactly can be proven, what exactly will stand up in a court of law, I don't know. Let's go see the lawyer tomorrow, like we planned, and see what happens."

Maybe she needed a hug. Collin moved toward her.

"Stop," she said. "Leave. *Now.*"

*****

In Julie's mind, two forces pushed and pulled. She knew, she knew all along, that she needed to do the right thing, without building hopes of financial gain. She knew that, but it had always been in the back of her mind -- Alternate Thought B -- there could be a lot of money coming her way. But, she had always managed to turn away, especially with Pastor Andy's help. His patient conversations calmed her mind.

Now, sitting in the lawyer's office, she couldn't really keep Alternate Thought B down any longer, it was doing pushups in her mind and her heart pounded at the thought of it. HH sat beside her. Julie could hear him breathing and wondered if he was about to have a heart attack and if he did wouldn't that be wonderful for her, the only heir, and then she said to herself *shut up*. She noticed her right leg, crossed over her left, swinging energetically, almost to the same rhythm as HH's breathing. Consciously she slowed the leg down, put both feet on the ground, and calmly folded her hands. She would pretend poise and calm even if she didn't feel it. She could hear the lawyer now, on the other side of the door, talking to his secretary, and Julie sensed the importance of the upcoming scene, and knew that she was about to blow it. *Oh, God, please remove this money-grubbing attitude from me, Help me to take the high-road in this situation and the rest of my life. Whatever you want here is fine with me.*

Chapter Thirty

Collin put on his best shirt, looked at himself in the mirror, frowned, and then took it off and put on an orange shirt, something Sandy bought him, an awful color, but an artist ought to like it. He smoothed down his thinning hair, checked his teeth, and went next door. Julie's bags were already on the front porch. He knocked. She looked glorious and fresh and he wanted to just touch her hair.

"You'll let me know what the doctor says about your wrist?" asked Collin as they walked to the car.

"Of course. I can hardly wait to have this splint off permanently. And see my friends. And my apartment! And Santa Fe!"

On the way to the airport, she talked nervously, spilling the words with excitement, talking about everything. Everything but him. "I'm so glad the lawyer and the court are going to figure everything out. I'm really quite tired of thinking about it. I don't like letting criminals get away with anything, but this way, HH and Van and that crazy art collector, they can all come to terms with their lives and I will come to terms with mine."

She stopped, or so Collin thought. He started, "I was wondering--" but she interrupted him, "I can hardly wait to get home." She carried on about the sky and the mountains.

We have sky and mountains here, he thought. And so it went, all the way to the airport, and there was Andy waiting for them at the curb. Thin, fit, cheerful, Andy. He helped Julie out of the car and took her bags. Fine, said Collin to himself, I've lost my chance. The only woman I've been the least little bit interested in since Jan, and I've lost. It's the pastor. She wants the pastor and he's a good man. What's the high road here? He parked the car and walked back to the tiny airport with a heavy heart, and found Julie and Andy at the gate, her bags checked. They leaned toward each other, deep in conversation.

He respectfully stood apart. When they turned toward him he smiled and said, "I'm glad you found a new painting style while you were here."

She hugged Andy and then she hugged Collin, and then she was off, through the gate. Would she ever return? He turned to Andy and they walked back through the airport. "Looks like the best man won her," said Collin.

Andy stopped and put his face close to Collins' face, making him uncomfortable. The pastor could be forceful. "God's winning here. She's leaving, searching for God, and that's the most important thing." And for added emphasis, Andy thumped Collin on his chest, and then said,

"You'd do well to follow her example."

*****

Collin climbed the steps to his front porch slowly and when he got to the hammock he sat and then lay down in one fluid tired motion. He listened to the birds; a plane buzzing overhead; and the ferry blowing its ten-minute warning.

"Dad?" Sandy spoke softly from the door.

"What?"

She quietly came out and curled up on the chair next to him. "Are you sleeping?"

"No."

"Were you sad to see her go?"

"What if I was, would that bother you?"

"No. Not at all."

"Really?"

"Really." Quietness.

"So, what are you going to do for the rest of the summer?" he asked.

"Actually I wanted to talk to you about that. I could continue working the odd jobs thing with Tyler. But something has come up."

"Like what?" he said, opening his eyes to look at her.

"I've really hated to tell you this, but I need to."

He knew it. She was sick. Or pregnant.

"Just lay it on me."

"You're not going to believe this, but my art history professor called me and wanted me to come work for him for the rest of the summer. He needs help organizing his files and slides for a worldwide lecture tour."

"What did you say?"

"I said the truth, which is this. This is the most precious summer for me. My dad and I are spending time together, and I didn't think it would work."

Collin sat up. "You didn't?"

She looked hurt. "How could you not value the time we're spending together?"

"Oh, Sandy, Sandy. Of course I value it. But you can't put your life on hold all summer and make me your project. Time moves. That's a wonderful opportunity he's offering you."

"You mean you wouldn't mind if I went?"

Mind? Getting her away from Tyler and getting her back to her education?

"Sandy, I'll miss you. But we've found each other, and that won't go away. Go on with your life. You may not get another opportunity like this. Call him back."

She threw herself at him with a big hug. "I'll miss you."

"I won't miss you. You're always bossing me around."

"You're my hero, Dad. What will you do without me?"

"Plenty. I've got projects. Like Tyler. He needs a strong hand and I'm it."

"Will you go to church? I heard you talking about it with Julie."

"None of your business. Go get packed. Leave an old man alone."

She got up and slowly went to the door. Without turning, she said, "Are you sure? I would be glad to stay."

"Go away."

"Is that any way to talk to your daughter?"

"No, but it's a way to talk to an adult, one that I love very much."

*****

Sandy smiled as she went in the house. She started packing and thinking about Seattle. It didn't seem so challenging now. She knew where to find a place to live, she knew the people she wanted to connect with. And her dad, her support, he was close by.

Building of the Kingdom Book Two: Singing Windows
Coming May 2017

About R. M. Rogers

A spontaneous, seeking, difficult, lovely woman – so says her husband.

Made in the USA
Charleston, SC
12 February 2017